To

staff U

Thank You for
your kind
help on the day

9ᵗ/ May/2012

a Sufi Love Story

RAZ

In the name of
Allah
ir–Rahman
ir–Raheem

Black Taj Mahal
a Sufi Love Story
©

This edition published in 2010 by

al-Oblong Books
P O Box 354
Burnley
Lancashire
BB10 4XD

for

UL HAQ
Art Education

ISBN: 1-905015-08-9

*British Library Cataloguing in
Publication data*

A catalogue record for this book is
available from The British Library

Contents

Non-fiction

A note on the illustrations

Artwork Praises the Creativity of the
Divine Being. The Ultimate Creator.
Allah. The Divine Artist.

You will find that in this book, each
drawing reflects the world
in a sub-abstraction. As of itself, it has
limited, non eternal reality.

Human eyes, being the screen to the soul
have not been depicted in any piece of Art
contained herein. In recognition and awe
of the Creator, who has placed a unique
soul in each person.

Allah is the Ghafur, *Forgiver*

The White Taj Mahal
As described by its Patron,
Emperor Shah Jehan:

'Should the sinful seek asylum in the white
marble enclosure of the Taj Mahal,
surely their sins will be washed away.
Just a glance of the Palace is enough,
for
both the sun and the moon shed tears,
in wonder:
how is it that in this mundane world, there is such an
adornment to display Allah's glory?'

The Black Taj Mahal
Some say this was the unrealised dream of
Emperor Shah Jehan.

Whether it is a myth or fact is not the point.
The metaphor of Black goes
towards the heart,
to Blackness of the Black Stone in Makka.
Like the Black Stone,
the Black Taj Mahal belongs
to another reality.
The fantasy of expectation is greater
than solid beauty on earth.

Allah is the Nur, *Light*

Razwan Ul-Haq

muhammad ur Rasul Allah

BLACK TAJ MAHAL

a Sufi Love Story

Preface

`

Noor (*knowledge*) + Kalandar (*insight*) = Reality

Kalandar (*perception*) + Noor (*rationality*) = Truth

Noor (*modern*) + Kalandar (*traditional*) = Timeless

Kalandar (*seeker*) + Noor (*sought*) = Union

'Verily the vision of a believer is a forty-sixth part of Prophecy.'

PROPHET
Muhammad

There she goes. Driving around in a powerful beast of a car, listening to heavenly verses. Her beautiful face shining in the twilight. Let me introduce you to Noor (she's uncannily intelligent too).

We begin our story right in the heart of the City of London. Noor jumps out of her red Ferrari. Straightens her flowing business suit. And gracefully pulls a sleek briefcase out from the boot.

'Have fun!' she smiles, handing the car keys to her PA.

'Noor. Why on earth can't you take your Ferrari to Bradford?'

'How many times do I have to explain? My family aren't loaded. I want to blend in,' with that she sits into a Toyota Corolla. Swiftly kicks off her stilettos.

As her PA parks the Ferrari, Noor reads a text and sighs: 'It's the boss. Needs to see me. An Emergency. So he says.'

'Which car will you be going in? You can't go in that one. I'll reverse back towards you.'

Noor pauses. 'No don't. Think I'll take the black Lambo instead.'

* * *

Bradford. No place could be more different from the square mile of London. An unusual juxtaposition of damp grey terraced houses remixed with Eastern colour. Little girls in shiny embroidered dresses contrast the unforgiving plain pavements. A sign on a silk shop reads:

No weapons of mass destruction in here
No bombs and no terrorists
Try 10 Downing Street instead

Visions are screens upon which are relayed pillars of Love. Find a place you feel baraka. Sit there. What lights descend into your heart? Do you see sparks through the vision of your soul? They are bubbling like fizz. Catch the inspiration. Learn from direct perception.

3   a Sufi Love Story

'When Allah created existence, He inscribed upon His Throne: *My Mercy has preceded My Anger.*'

PROPHET Muhammad صلى الله عليه وسلم

The Breath of the Passionate One, *Nafs ar-Rahma*, has spilt onto all things, all circumstance and abstraction. Stuff is absolutely loaded with it. Inclination to graceful mildness is in each air molecule you gulp down into your lungs. Feel it circulate in your blood.

The writer of this poster, Ameena, an unmarried twenty-something is bored behind the till. The sweaty smell of leather *khusay* and oft-tried *jootay* [1] amidst the jumble and litter of silk rolls is her daily environment. Reads a text. Then puts her gleaming mobile away, shouting loudly towards the back kitchen: 'Ami-ji. Just got a text from Baji Noor. She's going to be late –has to go back to the office.'

Her mother grimaces, 'Oh my poor child. I always knew London was a bad move. It is not a place for my innocent daughter. Ya Allah, protect her.' Ami-ji unhurriedly continues with the stirring. And wow, how the friendly fragrance of coriander, cinnamon and cardamom *et al*, can literally waft you out of Bradford and into a sunnier clime.

'It's not fun without Noor.' Dejected, Ameena turns away and begins to puts up wedding decorations all around the untidy shop floor.

'My child, don't worry. Your sister will be here soon.'

Ameena adjusts the speaker volume on her trendy phone as a Bollywood tune fades automatically into an American rap.

* * *

Noor briskly arrives at the office.

Located at the centre of the City.

Takes a lift to the top floor. But her senses are in Bradford.

My Allah. I should be with my family. She suddenly tastes the scintillating scent of Ami-ji's rice waiting for her.

An enormously built grey haired man is sitting in the most expensive office of the entire corporation, 'Ah my dear. Noorie! Nice of you to answer my call.'

Noor puts on sunglasses and runs her hand through her thick shiny wavy hair, *she hates him for his informal way and* that *name he uses for her: Noorie,* 'Mr Purves. Friday is always difficult for me. I was on the way to my parents.'

'I understand your commitments. Take a pew.'

She sits in the chair, oblivious to her, Senior Law Firm Partner, Stuart Purves is mulling over entries on her Personnel File:

Noor, 32, born: *Bradford. Pakistani heritage*

LLB (Oxford)

Languages: *English, Arabic, Urdu, Panjaabi*
Specialism: *Finance Law*
'Well?' Noor is slightly irritated by the arrogant manner of her line manager. *I'm glad I'm wearing sunglasses, soon he'll be trying to stare into my eyes.*

'I need you to look at this file for me –a New York Client needs it before close of play,' he slides a file into her fingers, deliberately touching the skin of her wrists.

She sighs. *Do I have a choice?* Then smiles at Purves, 'Don't worry, I'll sort it out.'

'Very good Noorie and as it's Friday night, a drink?'

'I'd love to but you know I don't drink,' Noor sighs, *so this is the real reason he's called me in,* 'and I really need to get to Bradford. I've a wedding to attend.'

'Not yours I hope?'

'No,' she turns away.

Purves frowns. 'Why so hasty? Like I said it's Friday night.'

She notes a touch of masculine menace in his voice.

'Noorie darling we work too hard. Sometimes colleagues need to gel together in the evening after a difficult week. I didn't promote you as my number two just to make phone calls.'

'You know I don't like to mix my private life with work.'

'Work? You're always working. Working. Working. Working. When we leave for home, you begin dealing in foreign exchange and the stock market. You've made a bloody fortune investing in shares haven't you? You've got nicer apartments than all of us and bigger diamonds than the Sultan of Brunei's wife.'

'I enjoy my work. I like life the way it is.'

Suddenly, Purves's mood changes:

'It doesn't matter what you like. This ain't Bradford. You're in Corporate Law now. To move on up you need to network. Plus. You'll love London's nightlife. Come out with me tonight.'

'I'm sorry I can't.'

'Noorie dear,' he flashes a disgusting brown stained toothy smile. His foul smelling mouth makes Noor stagger back a bit. 'I do feel you're always letting yourself down. We never see the real you. Do you know what you are doing? You're just feeding racism and anti Muslim feeling. In the office all of them say you don't come out drinking

'Allah will not be kind to those who are not kind to humanity.'

PROPHET Muhammad صلى الله عليه وسلم

Radiate compassion. Broadcast caring thought waves. Be considerate and impart raindrops of concern. We are under the aegis of the All-Kind Monarch, so let's reflect His insignia.

with us, as you're different. I know you don't wear those headscarf things, but you still need to blend in a bit more.'

She sighs and swallows hard.

'I think I might just be able to do a couple of hours later. Just give me some time to go home and get changed.'

'Excellent.' He shows her the door, stumbling over his own body weight, landing awkwardly. Flabs of infected skin peer out from under his opened shirt.

Noor sends a text:

'Salam. Ameena. ☹ Sorry can't make it tonight. Chotti bayn. C u 2moro insha-Allah.'

*   *   *

Early, very early next morning.

Somewhere in London.

The posh apartment's alarm clock bleeps out the call to Prayer. Noor is already at the prayer mat. Her forehead's on the soft expensive jai-Namaaz, a golden Mughal Musalla[2] sprawled on the white marble floor.

Inside her heart, she's exploding, *can't concentrate on the prayer. OMA, I should be at the preparations for my cousin's wedding. How I miss the love and warmth of family life. The visual honesty of cheap but functional décor and the reality of Ami-ji's hand ground herbs is more meaningful than this artificial worklife. Oh my Ami-ji! How I've let you down...*

She finishes prayer and takes off her silky scarf. Tosses it onto a white leather sofa.

She ponders about life, *am I better off leaving England? This is such an artificial clammed existence. As a child I would be chased by the village cat in the Panjaab[3]. Run through dreamy plains. Listen to Nana-ji's stories of Jinn, Black Magic and Paradise. The morning breezes. The lovely pavilion. Women were allowed to be daughters and sisters there. Not workaholics. Yet. Sigh. My extended family back in the Panjaab wouldn't have let me live alone in a million pound apartment.*

Her feline fingernails press a diamond encrusted ebony button on a wall and her hidden Italian Wardrobe swings open. More silk. A Red and Black Salwar Kameez. Her favourite. Her colours.

'He who is deprived of gentleness is deprived of good.'

PROPHET Muhammad صلى الله عليه وسلم

Fluffy love floats hearts and drowns weapons. The eyes of the Beloved creates a constant symmetry where the power of gentleness moves mountains.

Momentarily glances at a share price alert. *But not quite yet the right time to sell.*

Sigh, how I miss Bradford. A life of people who care for me. Look after me. Call me either Baji⁴, bayn or auntie. Here they call me by my surname. I have no other relation but that of a worker.

She smiles as her eyes spot the perfect diamond encrusted jewellery to go with her dress.

* * *

Stuart Purves pours red wine into an unwashed glass, he'd pocketed from the previous night's bar. It was the glass Noor had drunk from yesterday. *Only the girl hadn't drunk any wine.*

His flabby fingers worked astonishingly swiftly over his phone. Man, could he text.

'Noorie. Thanx 4 spendin time wid us last night. Had a wondaful evening. Wot u doin 2day? My yacht is free4u xxx'

He locates where she had placed her lips and he puts his prematurely aged cracked lower lip onto her lipstick mark. Looking over at the large screen blue-toothed to his mobile, he waits for a text response.

Text tone.

'Sorry. No can do. Must go 2 family weddin.'

' Will u b drinkin?'

pause

'U know I'm a Muslim.'

'I know lots of South Asian girls who drink y r u different? ☹ People may start thinkin u r terrorist.'

pause

'Look Stuart. Sorry, I hav to drive 2 Bradford. C U Monday ☺.'

His fist bangs onto the table, spilling the wine.

* * *

Ami-ji's eyes relax as Noor hugs her. She finally made it to her home. Mother's forehead becomes less wrinkly. Tears of joy emanate. 'Meri bayti! Noor! Aa gae ho!'

'Where are those who loved one another for My glory? Today I will shield them in My shade on the Day when there is no shade but Mine.'

PROPHET
Muhammad
صلى الله عليه وسلم

Living on this earth as we do, we must do our bit of loving. Turn broken living into a unified hug. As you express clean goodwill, detach your soul and hit the tangy target of your inner desire. Allah.

Ameena pulls at her carefully made up hair, 'Salam alaikum. We thought you were never goin' to be make it in time. How was traffic?'

'Wa alaikum salam. Traffic wasn't the problem Ameena.'

'Oh my dear baji! Are you missing London already?'

Noor makes a much used, well understood signal to her sister. *Don't want to upset Ami-ji. We'll talk later.*

'Baji! Why has the Ferrari been left in London? It would have looked perfect at the wedding! You could have at least brought the Lamborghini!'

Noor: 'I didn't want to attract any attention.'

She looks at Noor's dazzling face and her gleaming diamond jewellery, 'Baji, since when did you ever *not* attract any attention?'

Ami-ji places dish upon dish of food in front of her favourite daughter. Quietly, Ameena slips upstairs into her tiny bedroom.

She accesses Noor's electronic diary. She'd long convinced herself that it wasn't spying. Someone had to look after Noor. And Noor had trouble in confiding in anyone but that diary. It'd be updated. Religiously. And usually on her travels.

Eagerly she types in Rani786, the hacked password:

DIARY ENTRY

Saturday on motorway service station.
Euurgh. Last night was bloody awkward. I was hoping to be in Bradford in time for Mehndi 5 night. Pervy-Purves had other ideas. Just because they are not as close to their families as I am, why do I have to turn into an atomised workaholic alcoholic? Basically that's the rap. I can't believe I gave in and smelt wine and stared at by every gora6 there. Will Allah forgive me? Well, at least I left before things began to heat up. Does this only happen to Muslim women? Why are we caught in the middle. This morning I got a series of texts from the boss ending with one accusing me of being a terrorist. He must think it's so funny. Or is he threatening? Why is it so hard to read European men? Talking of men, I got eyeballed by two Asian guys just now. They're probably wondering why a Pakistani woman is out all alone bejewelled and decked out in her finest! If London is bad, why do I bloody live there? Don't know. Is it the sight of women married

off to uneducated villagers in Bradford? This isn't freedom either. You either have to be Slutty or Veiled to live there. Why is there no middle way? Doesn't the Qur'an want Muslims to follow the middle way?[7] I feel so out of place. Almost as if there is no place for a working reasonable woman. I hope and pray to Allah I'm not insulting the way of my parents. London and Bradford stink. But I must survive in both if I am to live. That's the point.

Ameena saves Noor's entry into her memory stick for later musings.

* * *

A group of young men stand outside the converted chapel. Now used for community meetings and weddings. The landscape of Bradford, along with the rest of Britain is changing rapidly, with the steady demise of church and pub, despite rapid East European migration.

Noor breathes in the air of expectation as the wait for the bride and groom begins. *My Allah, how colourful Bradford is this evening,* she muses. *It seems as if an Eastern mist has clothed them, such is the powerful effect of men in embroidered Sherwani and girls in bright bangles. Hired cars in the working class streets epitomize Panjaabi wedding mentality well. Spending weeks of hard earned money on Bentleys and other top end cars. To parade around town in. This one day they are Princes and Princesses. But didn't Prophet Muhammad, upon whom be peace, say that weddings which entail the least amount of expenditure are more blessed? Though the amount of money spent on this wedding day will remain in family memories, etched into their skulls 'til they die.* She contrasts this with her own situation, *I'm the opposite; I live a luxury lifestyle but deliberately transform into something common on my return. Am I so different to my cousins? It's almost as if I'm a Princess turned Pauper. The things I have to do just to blend in. My Ferrari and Haute Couture collections would just make me stand out like a seriously sore thumb. The things I have to do.*

'A believer mustn't dislike his wife. If there is a bad quality in her, he shouldn't linger on it but remain pleased with her positive qualities.'

PROPHET Muhammad صَلَّى اللَّهُ عَلَيْهِ وَسَلَّم

Life lived in Layla's love enlivens life. When admiring a rose look at the petals, smell the fragrance. Why just become fixated on its thorns?

'Noor, I saved you a seat. We'll be able to see both Dhoola[8] and Dhoolan from here,' an excited Ameena says through too much lipstick.

Noor's elegant strides don't go unnoticed. Heads turn and whispers begin.

'Aah the starters are coming,' Ameena pulls out a piece of cloth she brought from home to protect her older sister's dress.

Noor looks at the roasted chicken pieces and places one on her mother's plate.

'My beautiful Noor! Always the Rani! My daughter is dressed like a bride. You're the elder sister, but look youngest.'

'Ami-ji!' Ameena laughs, 'you're not supposed to be putting me down in my presence.'

'But she is so pretty, I feel so much for you. May Allah protect you from the Evil Eye.'

Noor whispers: 'Thinking of Nazar[9], why is that video camera constantly following me around?'

Through a mouthful of spicy kebab, Ameena: 'One of the highlights of Asian weddings, to be filmed whilst eating.'

Ami-ji, like all Muslim mothers hated their daughters being watched. Mutters some Panjaabi obscenities directed towards the motley crew of *filmmakers*. Pulls her headscarf around her head tightly. Angrily: 'Oh look! I can see Nana-Abu! Go tell him to send that ganda[10] camera man to the men's section.'

Nana-Abu could walk-waltz just as elegantly as his beloved grand-daughter. 'Noor, my dearest! I've been looking for you since this morning.'

'Sorry Nana-ji, you were out when I arrived.'

'My dear I wanted to share with you a wonderful little newspaper article.'

Noor's brown eyes shine.

'Noor, it's about the Mughals,' her grandfather is so excited, he's completely out of breath, 'it's about... about – a magnificent Mughal architectural project that was never finished.'

She smiles languorously towards her maternal grandfather, 'What was never finished?'

Nana-ji glows at the obvious interest she has in his words, 'Noor darling – you're not going to believe this, our ancestors were going to build a *Black* Taj Mahal.'

Ami-ji is unmoved, 'Both of you will have enough time to talk about things in Pakistan. Oh Noor, my darling, make sure you stay close to Nana-ji when you accompany your married cousins on their honeymoon. Children nowadays! There were no honeymoon-*shoons* [11] when we got married. At least they are going to Pakistan and not ganda Dubai.'

Noor and Grand Daddy aren't listening.. They're dreaming. Of a Black Taj Mahal.

* * *

'Do not belittle any good deed, even, if it be a cheerful face when meeting a brother.'

PROPHET
Muhammad
صلى الله عليه وسلم

It is often the little deeds that can create loveliness in you. Set the homepage of your soul to cheery gladness. Be upbeat. Soon, your signature wavelength will ripen into pleasant sweetness.

a Sufi Love Story

Silent voices are falling from every object, echoing the majesty of another
Being. What appears as a Lamborghini here is actually
BismillahirRahmanirRahim, Alhamdulillahi Rab ila-lameen (In the Name
of Allah, the Most Kind, the Lenient. All Praise is to God, Lord of the
Worlds). The Divine Name, ar-Raheem can be seen in front of the Ferrari.
The greater beauty is in the Face, unveiling the mysterious Art of Allah.

Chapter II

Lahore.   Once the Jewel in the Crown of the subcontinent. Former financial and trade metropolis of a magnificent Mughal Empire.

Stalls upon stalls litter the dusty roads. Underneath the haze of a blazing sun, street vendors make noisy sales. For centuries they had laid out their wares like this. Lahore has always been kind to traders.

A middle aged bearded man minds his array of books. Most of the time he reads the paperbacks rather than sell them. The rest of his precious time is spent mumbling to himself about his unlettered son.

'Tea?' a passing cha-walla's steaming sweet beverage cannot be resisted. Ever since *Pak Tea House* closed down, Lahore Literati had to make do with street tea.

'One cup Fareed-ji, shukria.'

Cha-walla: 'You seem glummer than usual, Ustadh-ji. Has Lahore lost all readers this morning?'

'My dear Fareed Sahb. Lahore lost itself years ago. It's not that. My blasted son..'

'Aaah, little Kalandar.'

'Kalandar is little no longer. The buffoon is almost thirty years old and still cannot read. How can I pass my book shop on to a complete illiterate?'

'Hmmm. Your Publishing Empire?'

'Quit fooling around. There he is. Walking towards us. Look at him dressed in rags. Deliberately trying to look poor when I attempt to appear rich to the rest of my family all settled now in London.' He puts the steaming cup of tea on a pile of books.

'I never could understand why they didn't invite you over.'

'Neither did I. But they couldn't even send me a single pound.'

'I heard one of your brothers wants a rishta for Kalandar?'

'Yes. Idiot Salman. Bara Bahi[12]. He wants Kalandar to marry his daughter. He has no idea about my son's lunacy.

'A believer does not taunt, curse, abuse or talk indecently.'

PROPHET Muhammad

How can there be discord in a lover's heart? Whoever is in passionate love swims in a sea of oceanic freedom where signs of Allah plaster every space. Nowhere and nothing to curse.

And spends too much of his time in that Black Cab making money in London.'

'Black Cat?'

'Cab. Not cat. A cab.'

'Oh. A taxi? Have you accepted the proposal?'

'Of course. Like I said earlier, how can I possibly pass on my business to my only son who can't even work out the titles people ask for. Shhhh. *Chup kar*. He's here.'

An unkempt, hairy face appears, 'Salam alaikum all. Thank you for the tea.'

'Oi, Kalandar. That cha's mine!'

* * *

In the corner of the Badshahi Mosque, a lonely figure. His eyes piercing. Black as a raven lost in a starless night. Not of this world.

Shaykh Junoon places his head on the hard ground, 'My Allah, show me the Splendour of Your Grace.'

A whoosh of air.

He looks to his left.

A grinning Kalandar.

'Oh Allah...' he gets up, 'and I thought perhaps a lovely Hur from Paradise would show up.'

'My Shaykh?'

'Kalandar. There is talk of a marriage proposal?' Shaykh Junoon changes the tone of the conversation.

'Yes,' Kalandar's eyes wonder past the Badshahi Minarets.

'Why the silence?'

'I was hoping you could read my mind's heart and tell me what my soul is fearing.'

'My dear young Mureed[13] this is the next step of the journey for you. You must now quit the Sufi assembly.'

'What!?'

'Your next teacher will not be Sufi, but will become one through you.'

'I don't understand my Shaykh.'

'In time you will.'

'In time?'

'No two love one another, but the better of them is the one whose love for his brother is greater.'

PROPHET
Muhammad

Feelings in your heart towards another human should be of brotherly love. Love is the flying albatross casting coolness upon the difficult desert of life.

'Yes, go to London. There you will meet someone who will transform you.'

'But.'

'Don't question me. Our bond is untied. I release you. You're no longer my student. I've dreamt that in a week's time your marriage visa will be issued. You must make haste. London awaits.'

Dumbfounded, Kalandar finds a spot of earth and looks towards the sky for answers.

* * *

'Nana-ji will I really be safe?'

'Meri pyari Noor, these are your first cousins, they will show you more respect and courtesy than anyone in England can. Have you forgotten Panjaabi hospitality?'

'Nana-Abu! All men have done is stare at me since we landed.'

'My girl! Don't blame the men. You're prettier than Mrs Universe.'

Noor giggles: 'Get real! I've got puffy tired eyes for lack of sleep! And her name is Miss Universe, not Mrs.'

Two broad shouldered freshly showered men appear in ironed Shalwar Kameez, smelling of freshly applied strong cologne.

'Baji, the driver is waiting. It is best to sightsee Lahore in the mornings.'

Noor sits in the car and is soon bored, 'Can't we walk outside?'

'Of course. *Yaha hi kharey ho jatae hae.*'

The two men are so busy talking to each other they don't notice her getting out of the car. She feels a presence drawing her behind a little cheap bookstall. A musky smell. She heads towards it...

Noor gets lost in the ever-narrowing aisles of the bazaar. In desperation trips over one of the thousand bits of broken stone. Falls headlong in a ditch. Clothes covered in filth.

She's now alone.

As she stands up, she forgets her bag.

I'm sure they parked their Toyota back there. Then she realises almost everyone in Lahore drives a light coloured Toyota. *Oh My Allah! I'm lost! No mobile and no rupee. What the hell am I gonna do?*

'Allah did not send me to be harsh, or cause harm, but He sent me to teach and make things easy.'

PROPHET
Muhammad

Remember that love is a bond between two people at a basic instinctive level. You need not show how competent you are, or expect recognition for your expertise or managerial expertness. Pavilions of love are comfy easy couches. Make life between yourselves easy.

She spots a policeman, 'Hey!'

He looks away from her, shouting at the top of his voice, 'Beggar! Move along!'

Then she runs into the hotel lobby of the Blue Diamond Continental Hotel, pleading in English.

The suited man solemnly points to a notice, 'Madamji jao! Didn't you read the sign? No vagrants allowed! Now they've learnt to beg in English. The miserable [14]gadey.'

Horrified, Noor realises she's absolutely smothered in filth and doesn't even know the address of her residence in Lahore. *Shit. Shit. Shit...*

Everyone will think I'm a scrounger. Already she can see kids poking fun at her, solitary men openly staring at her body as if it was an *Anarkali* commodity. *I'm an idiot, why wasn't I looking where I was going? Oh my Allah protect me and send Angels to guide me home.*

When she has almost given up hope, a man approaches her.

It's Kalandar.

Kalandar: 'Salam alaikum, yeh aap ka hae?'

Noor sighs relief at seeing something familiar. It's her bag and from the bulging look at it, the contents seem to be intact.

Noor is a professional and rebounds easily from a crisis. She returns the formality, 'Wa alaikum salam. Ji...'

Kalandar: 'Aap ka naam Noor hae?'

'Haa, ji haa...'

Kalandar smiles. He nods. He knows her name from the *shanakhti* card in her bag. Tells her that he's been looking all over the streets of Lahore. She dropped it near the ditch, but by the time he got there, she was gone. He had given up looking for her, but found her *accidentally*.[15]

When he hands the bag over, their hands touch. Suddenly he removes his hand.

At this action, Noor's forgotten her loss. No man has ever withdrawn his touch from hers with such speed and innocence. She senses his eyes searching her face. But in a decent gentle friendly way.

His aura changes. He becomes like a man who's rediscovered himself.

'But is it me or is it the bag?' she ponders.

Remembers where she is. She takes out her mobile.

Speaks to a distressed cousin.

He's on his way.

'Wearing silk and gold is not allowed for the men of my community but allowed to the women.'

PROPHET Muhammad

Man is man. Woman is woman. Feminine is known by a characteristic not manly; and vice-versa. True gold and silk lies in her difference to him. Difference is a pre requisite of paired love.

Meanwhile the perplexed but by now, utterly confident Kalandar has moved closer to her.

But the cousins are now here, running towards them. (She's tired and should really sit in the car.)

The sun brings brightness amidst the gloom of normality. Noor catches Kalandar's thoughtful words:

'Your name is in a poem...'

She turns around. Her luxurious hair creates glossy black waves against the Lahore landscape as a sudden gust crosses her face.

His eyes probe deep into hers.

'A Poet has written,' Kalandar says softly, 'has written your name...'

'My name means Light,' she finds herself saying.

As she is walking towards her cousins, she feels magnetised to him.

Noor begins to walk hesitatingly back to Kalandar, thinking, 'he's found me, not the bag.'

She senses the air between them becoming charged. Takes in the shock on his youngish scruffy face as she's nearing his presence.

Suddenly her cousin lashes out. 'Is this *mangta* bothering you?'

'Kuta da putr, ja.[16] Haraami.'

Noor is stunned as she's swiftly bundled into the vehicle.

Looks into the rear view mirror. Nothing.

She explains how she lost all her possessions.

Frustrated cousin: 'Why didn't you ask someone for a phone?'

'They all thought I was a beggar just like you thought he was. You know, that man –the man who helped me. The one you hit and swore at. When you can't trust any stranger, how can you expect anyone to trust me when I looked strange too?'

The car silently pulls out of the side street and onto the main road.

* * *

Noor has slept through two days, but is glad to have accompanied Nana-Abuji today. The drive may have been long and protracted, but gladly they're now at their destination. *Sheikhapura.*

She watches the tiny specks of buzzing insects against a Mughal monument in the almost open country. Oddly, there

'The perfume used by men should have stronger odour but no colour, and the perfume used by women should have a colour but less odour.'

PROPHET Muhammad

The fragrance of man is an invisible musk that remains with her after he leaves, whilst the woman's fragrance is enhanced in her intimate presence.

are no other visitors today and it all seems so isolated. Trees stand in ranks as if guarding the enclosure.

'This is it. Hiran Minar,' Nana-ji places his hand in Noor's.

Noor: 'Lovely. Just as I remember it. Nice sandstone upon a marvellous little lake. Built by the Mughal Emperor Jehangir, for his favourite antelope.' She picks up a luscious wild flower, which looks lovelier in her silky hands.

'Ah. You remember. You came here when you were barely five years old and you have the story etched firmly in your dear little heart.'

'Nana-ji, you forget you've been retelling the story over and over again on our way here.'

'Hmmm. And you wore yellow that day too. If only your grandmother was here.'

'Don't be sad,' she squeezes his aged hands and her heart drops but softens at the memory of the delightful poetess that was her Grandmother. 'Was Nani-ji really the daughter of an actual Mughal Princess?'

'My dear! We are direct descendents of the Mughals. Our forebears hid us and now all that is left is our past.'

'And what we have in our hearts,' Noor's voice is assuring.

'Indeed so. Indeed so. Have you brought an umbrella?'

'Is the sun shining too hard on you?'

'No child, it's about to start raining cats and dogs,' he says in perfect English.

She often wondered how he acquired his quirkily precise English accent and his mastery of many languages. Looks at the sky, 'Can't see any cloud.'

'Sniff the air. Dear Noor! Just as you gauge the atmosphere in your business meetings, I used to smell the air in the village to know when to run home. Let's take refuge.'

Nana-Abu continues: 'Hear that sound Noor? A peacock begins its call, announcing the beginning of a deluge. Rain, and bloody lots of it methinks. A sudden increase in precipitation is felt more acutely in the peacock than any other bird.'

They find a place to keep them dry. Noor gently helps her proud patriarch sit on a stone.

He smiles as the first drops of rain begin to fall, 'Aaah! This must be where Jehangir would have sought shelter too.'

The monsoon shower swings from a drizzle to a downpour. The smell of fresh love is in the air. Brought on by the sky's love of Earth? The Archangel Mika'il is the Heavenly Steed carrying the clarion call that is the life-giving liquid monsoon wind. Not even Jehangir's lake can compete with the enormous mirror of water surrounding them. Noor kicks off her sandals and walks knee high in water. Savouring the life, the energy, the buzz, the wonderfully complete sensation that is *being alive*. To be human on this earth. *Wow! What perfection. Prefer this to the boardroom any day! Do the poor here realise what they have and the rich in England what they are missing?* Her regal forehead is splashed by rainwater. And more diving water crunches the earth into submission. A mirage of a million virtual emerald tulips appear on the horizon, each cleansing the smoothness of the sky. 'Allah hu Akbar,' mutters Noor and recites verses from the Qur'an.

An antelope watches her. As if mesmerised by Noor's scent. The two are apart, yet she is floating sensually in the eye of the antelope. Her homestead.

* * *

In Lahore.

A crazy figure is dancing in the torrents of H2O.

It's Kalandar.

After tearing his shirt off, he paddles and constantly dives into muddy dirt and water.

All around him, the people who have taken shelter laughingly watch his apparently foolish antics.

My Allah. My God. My Life. Allahu! Allahu! Allahu! His constant cry. All is swirling spongy sprite-ness. He can't feel the rain but only light. Beams of maddening light. Forgets who or what. What's left is motionless movement. In his eyesockets there are waves of *being* echoing a thunder from an altogether different source. Feelings have died. Precariously close to actually killing himself, he races into the newly made river of a road. Colourful painted old trucks honk horns loudly. He swaggers and moves to their beat. *Huuuuuu! Huuuuuu!* His feet constantly miss the ground as the uneven Panjaabi tarmac cannot be seen. Sewage leaking into the water is gratefully gulped in. 'All is He! All is He!'

He can smell burnt kebab. Pushes all the wet rupee notes he has, under the dark skinned face of a man skewering the

'Allah loves to see the effects of His Blessings upon His servant.'

PROGET Muhammad

PROPHET Muhammad

Adorn the piece of Art that is you ...though do not look down with pride to those who have a form apparently less pleasing...

sizzling goat meat. Before he can say anything, Kalandar waves goodbye, 'Allah Hafez.' And is soon taking long strides eating kebab.

'Idiot! Kalandar! Making another show of yourself. ULLU[17] KA PATHA!' His father on a scooter doesn't stop but pulls his ear and drags him to one side.

Kalandar smirks and vomits in his father's face.

'No wonder Allah made alcohol Haram for Muslims. If you could drink, my Allah... Get out of your so-called intoxicated state. Just had a phone call. Your visa for London is ready. Record timing too. I'm sending you on the next PIA flight. And you can enjoy the rain there with your new bride. Maybe she could knock some sense into you.'

'But Abu-ji! I'm hungry. I need to eat three rotis.'

'Hai Allah. DAHN-GARR. Kitna paghal hae tu?'

'Ha! I am paghal.[18] I am paghal. Paghal for her!'

'SHUT UP! CHUP KAR KUTTIYA! KOI SUNN LAE GA!' his father looks around warily.

'For her! Her! Him! Him!'

He points to a hand drawn henna tattoo on his forearm. A drawing which somehow has resisted gallons of mucky water. It's an exact resemblance of *Noor*.

* * *

'Whenever kindness is in a thing it beautifies it, and whenever it is removed from anything, it disfigures it.'

PROPHET Muhammad

Have a kind attitude, for it will adorn your face, body and soul. The Beloved will love you more intensely.

The Divine attribute, Al-Majeed, eternally pointing to dazzling
magnificence. The meaning of life is to unlock the door to the
Super Being. Look inward and even your tear will echo His
Name. Your forehead will shine with light. Hidden as He is.
Such is Sacred Beauty. Attained after a long adventure.

21

Chapter III

Balmoral Castle. Set in beautiful woodlands. The Scottish home of the Royal Family. Tonight the Castle is lit. Buzzing with a charity dinner for the top 100 British Companies.

Prince Freddie, heir to the British throne is there too. His blonde short back and sides blend in well with his World War II smoking jacket. In fact the theme of the dinner is the 1940's. Gowns and suits with music reminiscent of the era fill the building.

Stuart Purves, his balding head covered by a terrible black wig, is busy texting during the opening deliberations. The MC is at the microphone.

'Hell is forbidden to those who are easy, flexible, modest and candid.'

PROPHET
Muhammad

Love's lightning doesn't emanate from a complex machine. Relationships that are open are heavenly.

'Noorie. U said u wud b here. ☹'

'Sorry Stuart, plane late. Got delayed at Airport.'

'Where are u now?'

'I'm at da Castle. Gettin out of taxi.'

'Wot r u wearing? A low cut 30's dress? xxx'

'A surprise.'

'☺ I like surprises. I hav a surprise 4 u too Noorie.'

'Wot?'

'A fully en suite bedroom, complete with his & hers xxx.'
Pause.

'Stuart. Taxi is 2take me bak 2nite.'

'Think it over.'

Prince Freddie stands at the podium and begins a speech in his characteristic clumsy manner. Stops bumbling and stares. His gaze falls to the back of the hall.

Other heads turn.

Noor is nervously trying to find Purves. She's wearing a glistening red Shalwar Kameez. In total contrast to other guests. *Have they never seen an Asian woman at their dinners before? It's vintage Mughal. Will do in any period. OMA just look how badly dressed all the women are...*

Purves waves to attract her attention and to show off to other guests (that he is *with* her). Noor is conscious that all eyes are looking her way. *Shit. Shit.*

Prince Freddie wipes the saliva from his mouth and finishes his speech abruptly.

As he sits, he whispers into the ear of an effeminate man to his left (Head of Security), 'Could you be a darling and discover the credentials of that rather attractive young woman who has walked in? Then have her escorted to the Rolls.'

'Yes sir. Emm. We had doubts on letting her in the first place. I can tell you who she is right now. She is a Pakistani descendant and therefore the risk to your person is high. It would be a risky choice. Prince.'

'Do those idiots who taught you dear –them blasted stooges at Sand Hurst know anything about anything? How can this fine young creature have vile tendencies? Now listen here darling, if I die with her in the Rolls I'll die a happy man.'

At Noor's table, Purves opens his mouth, his foul tongue slurping horribly.

'Oh! You are looking extremely ravishing tonight,' Purves touches her silk dress and his fingers gently jab into her flesh. In his excitement, his false tooth spits out onto the floor.

'Thank you,' Noor pulls her arm out of the way.

A muscular rugby player, lumbering awkwardly in an ill-fitting suit shows his security badge, 'Miss Noor? The Prince has requested your presence. He would like me to take you to his Rolls Royce for a drive after the event. He requires some legal advice.'

'Er,' cuts in Purves. 'I'm her superior. All business must come through me.'

'I'm afraid the Prince only requested Miss Noor.'

'So be it,' Purves grimly pours red wine into his already grubby goblet.

* * *

Kalandar is afraid. He hasn't ever ventured out of the Panjaab, never mind another country. He had been strip searched by Heathrow customs and now waits like a beggar for his soon-to-be-in-laws. He feels like someone may rob him any moment of his passport and the thirty pounds in his pocket.

'He who saw me in a dream in fact saw the truth.'

PROPHET
Muhammad

Meetings in the dreamworld have a reality. The breathtaking journeys to faraway places, the souls, species and jinn we encounter are actualities. *In the world of dreams see the future.* Déjà vu *before perception of skin on skin.*

But no one seems to be there except a family holding a large piece of card, which to Kalandar is totally incomprehensible.

But Kalandar is psychic. *Well, a bit.*

'Are you Uncle-ji?' he enquires, trying to redo the collars of an ugly 60s shirt that once belonged to his father.

'Ha-ji!' Salman suddenly hugs his nephew. 'Why did you stand there all this time? Didn't you read your name or recognise us from the videos we send you?'

'Oh, I was just confused.'

'*Oway!*[19] Nadeem, carry your cousin's bag,' he pulls at his moustache and points to the smiling woman who's about to hug him very firmly, 'this is your Auntie Atiqa.'

'Salam alaikum Auntie-ji.'

'Wa alaikum salaam. Hai kitna shareef. Kitni pyari dari hae aap ki.'

'Oh and this is,' Salman feels awkward.

Autie takes over, 'This is Farah.'

A thin pale girl spits out her chewing gum. Heavy music is blasting in her ears. In a show of disgust she folds her arms.

Sadness pours into Kalandar's heart. *Allah! Am I to spend the rest of my life with THIS? Yae to khusri lagti hae. She is wearing men's clothes... I can't see how I can live with her.*

'Nadeem! You and Farah go with his luggage. Your mother and I will bring Kalandar in the Cab.'

Once in the back of the car, Kalandar feels imprisoned. He looks out. All he senses is grey buildings, dog and pig. He vomits.

'Oway! What have you done? I've got morning shift tomorrow!'

Auntie-ji silences him, 'Koi baht ni. Now my sona putar, don't worry. We wanted to talk to you in private. Now people will say to you that Farah has a boyfriend. But it's all untrue-'

Salman almost crashes the taxi, 'Chup kar. Kalandar needs to relax a little before he goes to work. My son Nadeem is a trainee lawyer,' takes a sudden proud intake of breath, 'and he has managed to get you a job in the law firm where he works. It's in the City. The City! You will go daily with Nadeem and come back with him.'

'But Uncle-ji I don't know how to work in an office. I haven't studied.'

'The faithful are mirrors of one another.'

PROPHET Muhammad صَلَّى اللهُ عَلَيْهِ وَسَلَّم

The shortest, quickest way to dissolve your ego into nothingness is through love's looking glass. Look into the eye of your beloved and view your own behaviour. Travel the seven skies and reach Allah.

'Doesn't matter. You will be working as a Cleaner. The money is good and you can do taxi like me when you learn to drive.'

Auntie-ji, 'You are so lucky to have your Uncle Salman. Other Father-in-laws don't care at all for their sons. But you are one of our own. That's why we have arranged everything for you.'

The cab stops outside a Victorian terraced house.

Kalandar is shown to his room. A converted loft space with a tiny skylight. Uncle-ji: 'This, actually is Farah's room. You can use it now and both move in when you are married.'

* * *

Anyone who has ever hunted with the Royal Family inevitably end up in Balmoral. The hunt tonight is of an altogether different order. In the back of Prince Freddie's personal car, Noor is sitting comfortably. The car is smoothly negotiating the Caledonian grounds. Lochnagar is very quiet at this time of night.

'Sorry. I don't drink. Thanks for offering anyway.'

'Hmmm. I've always found drink a nasty old nuisance,' Prince Freddie smiles.

'You don't have to put the champagne away on my account,' Noor returns Freddie's smile.

'I notice the rather well groomed hair style and traditional Indian dress,' Freddie settles back into the leather seat.

'It's Pakistani! Not Indian,' laughs Noor.

'Oh, how rude of me! How could I be so uncouth. I hate them bloody Indians,' the Prince adds in a terrible accent, 'Pakistan Zindabad.'

Noor's black hair swing with her face, 'Aaah! So nice. How did you know that!'

'Oh, I know a lot of things.'

Noor brings her forefinger up to her chin, a dazzling diamond ring can be seen in the darkness of the night, 'Is it true that you have a hidden button on your person which causes Nuclear missiles to go into the atmosphere?'

The Prince puts down his champagne and laughs out loud.

* * *

'Give good news, guide people and draw near to one another.'

PROPHET Muhammad ﷺ

Love is the axis upon which the community should be founded. So spread cheer. Guide and have real love in your soul towards each and every independent soul.

My hand composing a reflection, itself a drawing.
This screen of souls deceptively depicted in 2D. Reality is Allah Al-Mussawar.
Artist of Art itself. Fashioner of soul fashion.

CHAPTER IV

Ameena reads the latest Noor diary entry:

*'Uf Allah! I'm so exhausted. Mentally, physically and guess what? OMA. My heart is doing funny things. Now I do like to keep my emotions in check but it's been a heck of a roller coaster. I keep thinking about a stranger during the night, the day and the times in between (though technically I know I'm slightly confused). An odd chap, I think he was a faqir or something, well, the one who found my handbag... I don't seem to be able to take him out of my mind. Did I want to reward him? Is that why? Am I guilty that my macho cousins abused him? Or was it something about the way his face shone when I looked at him.. I shudder to think what would have happened had I not met him, I would have thought all young men I've ever met in my life are twisted perverts. Anyway, the point today is not that, nor the fact that the real Pervert (Pervy Purves) had booked some luxury suite, doubtless to lure me into his smelly underpants. No. How often does a girl get asked out by a Prince? No joke. I have just come out of a private encounter with Mr Heir Apparent!! None other than Prince Freddie himself! He was soooooooooooooo charming and I suspect he felt as comfy as I did in the back of the car. Oops! I didn't mean it that way. We **were** in the back but only giggled. I have his private mobile number and his personal e-mail address. Judging by the way his eyes were glazed over, I'd say it's a fair bet he wants to know me better. He even laughed that I was as regal as a Princess. Little does he know that I've got Mughal blood flowing in my veins. Good times ahead?'*

Ameena spills most of the *Kashmiri chah* she was drinking, and falls headfirst onto the floor. Just about avoiding concussion.

* * *

'There is a reward on account of every living thing. A man who quenched the thirst of a hungry dog was forgiven his sins.'

PROPHET Muhammad ﷺ

Love should spread far and wide and each creature is a creation of Allah. Shed your love upon all.

'Do not hate one another nor contend with one another. Slaves of Allah, be brothers.'

PROPHET
Muhammad
صلى الله عليه وسلم

Cram your life with sparkling love. Compete not with worldy possessions and fame. Love those who have more than you and those who have less. Love is status without rank.

'So this is the new boy? Huh?' the Gujerati Supervisor looks at Kalandar with a certain amount of disdain and scratches a mole on her cheek. Then picks at her ears.

'Your hours are fixed. Don't ask for more. You work shifts with *no* overtime. Do you know what this is?' she holds up a vacuum cleaner.

Kalandar replies: 'Hoover?'

'Not a Hoover. Why are all bloody Asians docile?' she looks to the ceiling with her own Asian eyes. 'This is a Vacuum. With this you do floor cleaning. Theek [20] hae?'

'Ha ji.'

'Don't bloody Ha ji me! Only speak English when I am around. Theek hae?'

'OK.'

'You see this thing on a wire? It's called a plug. It goes into a wall on a socket. They have proper three pronged sockets, not those crappy little twin ones back home. Theek hae? You must always say 'excuse me' and never walk in front of any staff in the building. You empty all bins, and do the latrines – they call them toilets here. I inspect toilets every two hours. Thaek hae?'

'Thaek hae.'

'If you speak your own language to me once more you're sacked. And I don't care if your cousin is a Trainee Lawyer. Thaek hae?'

Kalandar still has no idea what to do, so just starts cleaning.

She watches him suspiciously, and then goes for a coffee and a chat with a group of Sikh housewives.

He feels so alone. *I didn't come here to sweep the floors and sleep in a dingy little room.* He picks up a banana skin. And shoves it in the bin. *Oh-uh. I'm the one who has to clean the latrines. How will I know where they are? I'll leave those to the end.*

As he is walking downstairs, he can smell an intoxicating fragrance. Enquiringly, he peers out to see who the source of the mystery scent is, kneeling down to pick up litter. Doors of a lift are already open and a sweaty faced, hideously grinning Purves walks out. *Oh-uh, this can't be the perfumed one!* He hears a familiar female voice behind him. *Ya Allah!* Noor floats past, black shiny locks flowing over a pearl white business suit. Even her attaché case is colour co-ordinated.

Kalandar quickly swirls, reminiscent of a *Osmanlari* Dervish, before she can spot him. *It's her!* The joy of seeing Noor is eclipsed by his status as a cleaner. *Oh-uh! What will she think of me? A dirty job. Cheap clothes. This isn't me. My Reality is far more significant. How will Noor recognize my real soul? I need to hide...*

'Noorie. That was a good meeting. I really think we've got the contract. Your stunning good looks always bring in classy punters,' Purves looks at his wristwatch, 'see you at the Case Meeting at 4pm.'

'OK,' Noor grips her bag tightly, *why do people ignore my intelligence and skills and think it's only my appearance that's got me to where I am?*

Something makes her stop in mid-thought. An abruptness. Can smell musk. A musk that takes her back to her childhood. Her soul picks up an extra signal. She looks over her shoulder.

But Kalandar has already gone.

* * *

The *grand* things about *Grand Daddies* is that they still use landlines and sit with their reading spectacles, writing memento aplenty on slips of paper when they are excited academically.

'Oh my beautiful Rani! The Black Taj Mahal must have existed. They've discovered great big blocks of black marble near the site in Agra!'

'Aaah!'

'The Black Taj Mahal was going to be the resting place of guess who? Shah Jehan himself. Right opposite the mausoleum of his beloved Mumtaz. Isn't that sweet?'

'So romantic!'

'To think they were our actual ancestors.'

'I've always found that in London, people are always guessing my origin.'

'My Rani, let them! You've got genes from every corner of the world.'

'What do you mean?'

'The Mughals had Harems where there were Turkish, Central Asian, Chinese, Arab, Bangali, Indian and African women. Don't believe Orientalists.'

'The Western Scholars of the East?'

'Oh, out of kindness return the bird's eggs to the nest.'

PROPHET
Muhammad
ﷺ

In one incident a distressed bird whose eggs were taken troubled the Prophet deeply. Show care for the feelings of those who are hurt. Affectionate opulent love will transform their situation.

'Yes, only I wouldn't call them scholars. The Harems weren't dens of wickedness. Far from it. They were places where the next generation of Rulers was genetically created. Unlike the Western Kings, they did not breed into themselves. Oi! Noor I can hear you giggling.'

'Sorry Nana Abu-ji!'

'Yes. You're the product of a wide DNA. The finest gene pool was available to the Mughals and also the Osmanlari in Turkey. Why do you think you move like a Princess without actual training in Court Etiquette?'

'Nana-ji, you're making every hair on my neck stand up. It answers so many questions. But I'm not a Princess.'

'You're not just royal blood my Rani. You're the finest.'

'Oh Nana-ji, I've got to get off the phone. I've got a meeting soon. Will speak later tonight.'

'Make sure you cook something. Don't rely on restaurants. Remember what happened to me in Karachi?'

'Nana-ji I hear that *kahani* everytime! I *do* cook.'

'And, you're a superb cook too. Khuda Hafez my Rani.'

'Khuda Hafez. Sab ko salam daena.'

* * *

It's leaving time for all staff. Kalandar is waiting for his lift in the posh foyer. He is wearing an oversized hooded coat that teenagers wear above his work trousers. He looks every part the cleaner.

His supervisor, 'I know it's your first day *int* it? Doesn't mean you have to show how keen you are. Tomorrow leave at 4pm. The goray don't like us milling around. Thaek hae?'

'Oh. I'm waiting. For Nadeem, inshallah.'

'So keep waiting for him then.'

A lift opens.

A whiff of perfume and Noor strides out majestically. Like two thorns at her side, Purves and Nadeem follow eagerly.

Kalandar turns around and covers his face. Beads of sweat perspire out of his jangled pores. *I hope she doesn't see me... oh Allah, oh Hafez, oh Protector. Please don't reveal my state.*

Thankfully Nadeem walks straight past and says goodbye to Noor as she goes into her waiting Ferrari. Purves is

'Do not envy one another.'

PROPHET
Muhammad
صَلَّى اللهُ عَلَيْهِ وَسَلَّم

If you are truly engrossed in shimmering love, your insides will shine to the extent that envy finds no space to grow. Silver rings of sympathy and flashing bangles of light will adorn your radiant wrists and fingers.

disappointed. He was hoping she'd take him somewhere special.

Kalandar watches the smile she flashes at Nadeem and the way he hand-combs his hair after her elegant exit.

Nadeem sees Kalandar and waits for Purves to be out of earshot.

'Oi. Kalandri! Yaha kukar jaisay kahrae ho. Don't ever let my workmates see me with you. Tomorrow wait outside. I can't believe I let Dad talk me into giving you a job. I've got no chance of gaining permanent employment here if they see me with an uneducated tramp.'

Quietly, Kalandar accompanies him. He can't read the signs at tube stations, and even if he did, he'd still get himself haplessly lost.

* * *

24 hours whiz past.

It's raining in London. Kalandar has finished his second day. As per Nadeem's order, he waits outside.

Noor is reading Nana Abu's recent letter. He sends her his thoughts now and then. Letters are so much more personal than e-mails. *Some say England is a wet and horrible place. A Muslim traveller who visited Olde England once commented that parts of it were colder than Siberia. However many other modern Muslims have found the rain to be symbolic of Allah's baraka and the gardens indicative of Jannah, Paradise itself. And the Brits, on the whole, are a decent lot even if they are somewhat odd,'* she puts the letter back into her bag and continues downloading romantic pictures of Mughal Princes and Princesses. She's e-mailing them in response to Prince Freddie's request. As she is thinking about how Freddie would react to the miniatures, one picture makes her remember Kalandar. A warm feeling in the centre of her chest. She stretches her legs and inadvertently lets out a sigh which makes Nadeem, (who is supposedly learning Finance Law from her) jump nervously.

'Miss Noor, would you like a cup of tea?'

'What time is it?'

'Er. 6pm.'

'My PA will be coming in with some tea shortly.'

'The believer is guileless and generous while the corrupt is devious and miserly.'

PROPHET Muhammad صَلَّى اللهُ عَلَيْهِ وَسَلَّم

Be frank, mellow out, open your hands with twinkling love and generosity. Whoever wants to ruin self with sophistry may seem to progress in this world.

"Hey!" Look closer. Do you see what I see?

31   a Sufi Love Story

Nadeem: 'I'm going to get a cup for myself, I'll grab one for you too.'

'Thank you.'

'Do you ever wonder what it would be like if the Mughals were still in India?'

The question throws Nadeem.

'Sorry Nadeem. I was just thinking out aloud. Oh my Allah!'

'What is it?'

'It's raining. In fact it's chuckin' it down!'

'Now I know you're from Bradford. Your accent sometimes comes through.'

Noor giggles, 'And sometimes other things come through too.'

Nadeem, 'Like?'

'Oh, just playing with words. Didn't mean anything specific.'

She looks out of the window, 'Aaah. Look down there in the distance! There's a poor homeless man standing outside. He must be frozen. Get my umbrella and take a cup of tea for him too. Poor chap, he must be shivering. Give him this,' she presses a twenty pound note into his hand.

Nadeem stands up quickly. He wants to be her *Knight in Shining Armour*. He obliges. Happily running outside. He can feel Noor watching over him.

His footsteps slow down abruptly as he realises:

It's Kalandar. Wet through and through.

Having a quick glance over his shoulder, 'Kutiya! What the hell are you doing standing in the road?'

'Aap ne yeh hi kaha tha.'

'I told you to go *away* from the office. Not loiter near it in full view of everyone. I can't believe it. You've been spotted by them,' Nadeem then calms down realising Kalandar's helpless state, 'now please, you must go. Find some shelter. For goodness sake you'll catch a cold. This isn't Lahore. Oh. Here's some tea and some money. Look, there's a café there. Wait for me in there. Please.'

Nadeem walks back into the room, 'I've done the deed.'

Noor crosses her arms, 'What deed did you do?'

He has never seen an overbearing Noor.

'You shouted at him. You were so rude. And you're supposed to be a Muslim. How dare you insult God's creatures. Are you ever thankful of Allah's bounties? The Qur'an says that *the good are those who feed the poor.* If

---

'Someone who eats with his servant, rides a donkey in the market, and ties up his sheep and milks it is not arrogant.'

PROPHET Muhammad صَلَّى اللهُ عَلَيْهِ وَسَلَّمَ

When glowing love showers secrets in your heart, continue your normal routine, and don't slip into Satanic pride.

you want to be successful remember those less fortunate than yourself young man.'

Nadeem angrily looks at her fashionable clothes and then turns away disgustedly.

'I know what you are thinking. How could I talk about Muslim issues and not be dressed traditionally. Well Nadeem. Nadeem, this world is full of surprises.'

His anger subsides. There was something very soothing in Noor's mild tone.

Noor: 'You're not just another trainee. You're like a younger brother to me. I only want you to become a better person.'

He gazes into her melting eyes.

Meanwhile, someone has just been kicked out of the café for bringing in a cup of tea.

It's Kalandar.

He roams around looking for shelter. But quickly loses track.

He is now lost in Central London in the pouring rain.

* * *

Two hours later, Noor is working late.

Salman's black cab has returned from dropping off a Kurdish diplomat in Soho.

Nadeem barks into his mobile, 'Sorry Abu ji! I can't find Kalandar.'

'Kutayaah. How could you lose him in your office?'

'I told him to wait in a café.'

'Oway! Kitni gandi advais di tu nae. He can't go around bloody cafés drinking coffee. Is ko kharaab karna [21] hae? You wait where you are and I'm coming.' His black cab begins to break the speed limit.

Noor is somewhat surprised but not altogether shocked to find an e-mail from Personnel, 'Due to company restructuring, we regret to inform you that your position is under review.'

Purves walks in with two plastic cups of horrid vending machine coffee.

'Stuart. Have you recently talked to HR?'

He hands over a cup to her, making sure his unwashed fingers touch hers.

'Sorry?'

'Give gifts and you will love one another.'

PROPHET Muhammad ﷺ

Material possessions aren't real. Still, in this world of objects, continue to spread your effervescent love in the form of manifested presents wrapped in the atoms of your hands.

Noor: 'I just got an e-mail saying my job's under threat. Do you know about it?'

He shrugs his shoulders, 'All I know is that a certain someone is beginning to annoy me.'

She gets the point. 'Don't you think your game has gone a little too far?'

'Game? What game? You're the silly girl playing games. I chose you to come to Balmoral and how do you repay me? By bunking off with Prince Freddie.'

'That's not fair Stuart.'

'Look. Don't you ever forget who put you where you are.'

'I can prove to HR that my role is crucial to the success of the company. You said it yourself.'

'Said what Noorie?'

'That I bring in new clients. That I'm good. That-'

'I can't remember anything. You'd better have something substantial to say to Miss Baxendale when you meet her.'

'Who?'

'She's Head of the Firing Squad, if you see what I mean. She also happens to see me now and then.'

He leaves her.

Noor sits and sips a glass of water. *I need to detach my emotions. I mustn't fall into despair. Oh Allah! Bring me clarity. I need your help.* Sighing heavily, she looks out of the rain-clad window and watches a frantic Nadeem get into his Dad's taxi.

Salman's anger fills the interior of the grand vehicle.

He sits in the back, too scared of his Dad.

After a good half hour of Panjaabi swearing, they locate a trembling man cowering under a large tree by the side of the road.

It's Kalandar!

Uncle-ji Salman: 'Oway! Oway! Eedar aao!'

The Black Cab takes the trio home.

Auntie-ji stops worrying and blesses Kalandar with her hand, 'I've made you some cha. Come and have some garam garam pakoray.'

Much later. In his room, he takes off the wet clothes and remembers how rainy cloudbursts would give him freedom. Here in London, he seems to be running away from once friendly raindrops. Rain – the baraka. Baraka of Allah.

* * *

'Modesty is also a branch of faith.'

PROPHET Muhammad

Humility and shyness before the Beloved increases intimacy. Confidence can only do so much.

Kalandar has some time to kill the next morning. He can't read or write but has a gift for drawing. He draws an almost photographic likeness of Noor on the back of some waste paper.

Whilst cleaning the boardroom, he absentmindedly leaves his Art behind.

He carries on upstairs.

Noor is about to meet with her Union rep to discuss the recent HR problem. She's booked the boardroom for the meeting.

Finds the drawing.

Stunned. Who would do such a wonderful thing? Who is capable of drawing such a liquescent image of her warmness in an uncanny spiritual way?

Momentarily loses her bearings.

Needs to go to the toilet quickly.

But Kalandar is cleaning them.

Hastily she edges ever closer.

Kalandar wipes yet another loo seat.

She finds a sign saying 'Male cleaner' upside down as she's about to enter.

Wonders if she should wait or go inside. *But she does have an effect on men.* So decides not to get a male excited in a toilet. So holds back.

Something makes her hair stand on her neck. Some musky fragrance. Remembers the drawing...

She takes out the portrait of her from her handbag and gently unfolds it. Her forefinger feels the pencil strokes.

Kalandar receives sensational vibes: as if someone is touching part of him.

He needs air.

Sweat pours from his forehead.

She moves away as she hears footsteps coming out of the toilet.

He senses a friendly aura. Emanating from all directions? *But it's just a washroom.*

Her face freezes as she recognises his eyes.

It's Kalandar.

* * *

'Modesty brings nothing but good.'

PROPHET Muhammad

The ornament to bring about beauty isn't revealing clothing, but a modest persona. You'll find zingy love inside plain clean elegance but flatness behind those who reveal the skin of their forms in public.

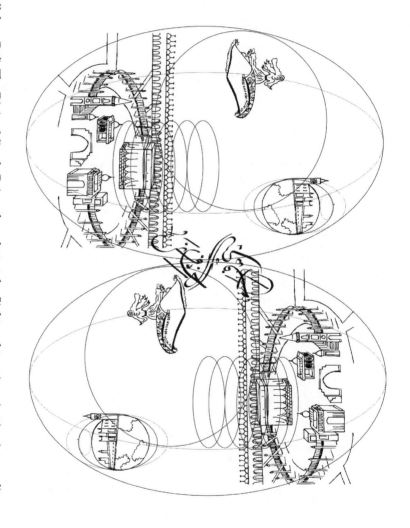

Allah ar-Rafi. The Divine Miracle Raises thought to take flight and turn imagination into reality.

36

Chapter V

Radio Pakistan:

'Salam alaikum. We regret to inform all citizens of the Islamic Republic of Pakistan that the Anglo-American invasion of Pakistan has no UN mandate. Pakistan will defend its territorial integrity. We urge all independent freedom loving countries to support us in our hour of need.'

Radio India:

'Good evening. The President of India, whilst welcoming the invasion of terrorist sites in Pakistan is becoming increasing concerned as to the new instability upon India's Western border.'

BBC World Service:

'In a joint statement, the Commander of the joint forces in Pakistan has said that phase one has been accomplished. Karachi and Islamabad have been secured. We are awaiting news of the battle in Lahore.'

Meanwhile in London.
A long protracted silence as Noor and Kalandar stand as if looking into a mirror.
Noor smiles, 'It's so nice to see you. I had no idea at all you worked here!'
Kalandar manages a lopsided grin, 'Salam alaikum Noor.'
'Wa alaikum salam. You remembered my name!' she looks down shamefully, 'I never did ask you what your name was.'
'But you still remembered me.'
Another long silence.
'Do you know, I've worked here for over a year and I've never noticed you till now!'
'Oh. I've only just come over to England.'
She notices him trying to hide the bucket and wet cloth behind him.

'The swiftest supplication to be answered is the supplication of someone for another person who is not present.'

PROPHET
Muhammad

Make dua for your beloved in secret.

a Sufi Love Story

Noor averts her gaze, and diverts his obvious embarrassment of the present by focussing on her own remorse, 'I wanted to apologize for the reprehensible behaviour of my cousins. I'm so sorry you got hurt trying to help me.'

Kalandar: 'No. I'd forgotten it. Honestly.'

'Well I've never got over how my family treated you. I wanted to say sorry and thank you for helping me out at a difficult time. How about a cup of tea together? When do you have your break?'

'Break?'

'Yes. Coffee break. Tea Break.'

'I don't have any break.'

'Oh.'

'When's your lunchtime?'

'It's ok as I have *naashta* before coming to work.'

'Oh my Allah! You mean you've been here since breakfast and haven't eaten anything at all?'

'I don't get hungry.'

'That's not the point. Come with me right now.'

'But Supervisor-ji is not going to be happy. She will be inspecting the toilets in a short while.'

'Look, all employees are entitled to a break.'

She leads him to her office.

A wide-eyed, agitated Nadeem watches them both.

She shuts the door behind him, 'I've just phoned the Cleaning Shift Manager. She said she'll look into it. In the meantime you're coming with me, there's a lovely café nearby.'

Kalandar: 'I went to one yesterday. They kicked me out. What is it with London?'

'Kicked you out. Whatever for?'

'I had a cup of tea in my hand.'

'Oh you can't take drinks with you into restaurants.'

She freezes in horror. Remembers sending the tea.

'Were you standing in the rain yesterday? Why? And do you remember who gave you the cup of tea?'

'Oh,' he suddenly remembers Nadeem not wanting to be identified as his cousin, 'oh. I like the rain. A nice friendly man gave me the tea drink.'

Noor isn't easily fooled. *He's protecting Nadeem. But why?*

* * *

The converted loft is peaceful that night.

Kalandar is too absorbed in Noor to listen to news and is sweetly oblivious to what's going on in rthe world. He has no idea of the Pakistani distress around the globe as people cry, scream and phone relatives. Kalandar contemplates her beauty as he gazes at the moonlit starry night through the skylight. Sketches Noor's portrait, amongst the piercing stars with the quill of his eyes.

* * *

Next morning,

'Oway! Hamara kiya hoe ga?' Uncle-ji Salman has taken the day off.

He reads out the lead story of a tabloid, 'Britain on brink of Civil War? Five bomb blasts in three hours have ripped the peace of our tiny island. As fears of more attacks grow, the PM has done nothing to assure the peace-loving majority. He continues to appease the Muslims by insisting terrorists have nothing to do with Islam.' He looks up. Makes an angry face. Continues reading very loudly: 'We are experiencing Jihad on our shores. We know it is coming from the Mosques.'

Auntie-ji looks to her husband:

'Oh don't read anymore,' she pours desi cha from the pan into a mug, 'my poor putr Kalandar. Your Abu-ji is in Lahore where all the fighting is taking place.'

Nadeem is talking with Kalandar in a hushed tone, 'What the hell were you doing in Noor's office yesterday? Thought you'd have the decency to tell me.'

'Nothing.'

'Jhutta. Don't lie to me. You were there for quite a long time.'

Kalandar plays with his half-fried egg. Swirling his toast, as his heart is pumping with fear and love.

'I don't like people who refuse to talk to me,' Nadeem adopts a threatening posture, 'I can see you like her. If Abu-ji finds out, you can forget all about the rishta with Farah.'

'Allah does not look at your bodies nor your forms, but He looks at your hearts and your actions.'

PROPHET
Muhammad

Love must not depend on the form of the body but the light of the soul. Such incandescent light beautifies the face.

Kalandar looks over to Farah nodding her head to rap music whilst eating soggy cornflakes.

'We could send you back to war-ridden Pakistan. What the hell were you and Noor talking about?'

Kalandar stirs at the mention of her name. 'She said I needed a break.'

'So she took you out to the café? I saw it all out of the window,' he looks in disgust at Kalandar's frightening mop of hair and compares it to his own styled neatness.

Kalandar is psychic, *well a bit*: 'There's nothing going on between Noor and me.'

'No. You're too dark skinned, too *kala*, for any girl to be interested in you. Just don't let me catch you with her again.'

* * *

The office.

Noor sees Kalandar but he doesn't seem to have made eye-contact with her.

'Kalandar,' she whispers softly as he is cleaning the bin by the photocopier.

She observes his eyes are full of natural kindness. But his face remains frozen.

Noor sighs as he walks past her.

Kalandar wipes the tear from his eye. His shaking hands clutch a strand of hair he found on Noor's desk. *I have to keep away from Noor. Otherwise Nadeem will tell Uncle-ji Salman and everything will turn into a mess. How can I tell her that?*

They say the Arch-Angel Mikhail has never smiled once since Hell was created. The air seems laden with mourning angels all around their auras.

Noor sits quietly at her desk. *Are all Panjaabi men so eccentric? What is wrong with them?* Kalandar seemed so different. His eyes say one thing but his mannerisms another. Does he not want to talk to me? Is it his interpretation of religion? Does he think it a *guna*, a sin to talk to me? *Oh well, Kalandar, I don't want to make you unhappy. If you want to keep your distance, then do so. I won't hurt you.*

'People will enter the Garden whose hearts are like the hearts of birds.'

PROPHET Muhammad

Scintillating lovers become unchained and fly in the air with trust in Allah as birds.

Her PA runs into the office, 'Noor! Have you heard the news? You're all over the papers!'
'What?'
Purves bounds in, out of breath, 'Freddie. It's Prince Freddie. He's told the press about you and him having an affair.'
'He can't have. We're not having an affair. Only a friendship.'
Purves leans ungracefully on her table, his podgy tummy bounces with his unswift movement. He looks away from Noor's hands and then to her covered legs, 'Huh!'

* * *

Kalandar finds weekends boring. Endless Urdu Satellite news fills his days. His nights are empty. He thinks of Noor and nothing else. Not even Pakistan.
Talking of Pakistan, Uncle-ji Salman has just entered his lounge. 'Owaaaay! Turn the TV down, I'm sick of hearing what the goray are doing in Lahore. May Allah destroy their countries!'
Auntie-ji: 'Don't be so vile! You goat, *we* are living in their countries.'
'This country is going to have a Muslim Queen! Why do Pakistani women not read decent English newspapers?'
He throws them today's tabloid. The gutter paper's front page: 'Prince Freddie admits going out with Muslim woman.'
They hurriedly switch channels. Footage of Freddie with Noor at a royal engagement is flashing all over.
Noor's happy expression is wonderful.
Infact, *so wonderful* that Kalandar's heart misses a beat. He puts his hand on his heart and vomits upon their carpet.
'Owaaay! Owaaay!'
Kalandar's half open eye watches as the television stills show Prince Freddie's arm clearly around Noor's tiny waistline.
Kalandar's anger overwhelms his passion. He loses consciousness.

'A good word is charity.'

PROPHET
Muhammad

All illuminated lovers use good words. Choose wonderfully colourful metaphors and speak well to the Beloved. Talk beautifully. Words need not be artificial, nor detached from reality. Let your heart talk. More hypnotic than synthetic words of a mind magician.

41   a Sufi Love Story

* * *

Bradford. Noor has arrived from London.

She's at a really posh hotel.

Noor smiles at the admiring waiter. She's not comfortable alone. Her sister is late. And already young men are fancying their chances. But, why has Ameena left Noor waiting?

You see Ameena is busy reading Noor's recent diary entry:

'It's such a rush of adrenaline travelling the length and breadth of Europe with Prince Freddie. He's beginning to hold my hand now. Ouch! I think he's a little annoyed that we haven't gone to bed yet. Double ouch! Hmmph. I'm going to have to stop our relationship –it's gone too far. He loves me, I know that. But I just can't love him. I feel so sorry for him. How will I be able to say goodbye? He's such a lovely character. Well, next week Freddie's taking me to India. To see the Taj Mahal. There I'll tell him there's not going to be romance between us. We'll have to be friends – and only friends. What of Kalandar? He's moving everything in my heart, mind, soul and even body! Ooops. Marriage – I've never considered it until Kalandar came along. And how I used to be so against British born women marrying Pakistani men from abroad. How one man has totally altered my view of the world! He's so helplessly naïve. Love his eyes. His honesty. Kalandar. Mmm. The name brings a butterfly fluttering to my little heart. I think I'm in love.'

A text: 'Ameena where the hell r u??'

She races to the restaurant.

Disappointed men watch her sit opposite her sister. Some of them brighten up: she's at least not with a man.

'Ameena I'm so glad you agreed to this.'

'Baji! This is the first time you've not come straight home from London. What's up?'

The waiter brings their roti.

He takes an agonizingly long time to lay the table.

'It's Prince Freddie. He wants to visit our shop.'

Ameena: 'Oh shit. Where will you two sleep?'

'Meenie! Quit foolin' around! Our lounge is tiny. How on earth will we entertain the future King of Britain? And, you know Amiji and Abu can't speak English properly.'

'We shouldn't be ashamed of our parents Baji..'

'I'm not ashamed. Ameena, listen. I feel like I've been dropped into an impossible situation. Think of media interest. The security. Oh my Allah – what about Nana-Abu-ji? I'm not so worried about what Freddie thinks of my background. I'm more concerned about the effect on Amiji if they get badly treated by the people around us. Ever since the invasion of Pakistan, there is ill feeling between the British establishment and *aapne*. We'll be outcast as sympathisers. I don't want that to happen.'

Ameena sips her orange juice quietly.

* * *

Monday morning. And yes, *London*.

Purves has called Noor to his office.

'Right. I see you've called in your Unions?'

'Please don't seem so surprised Stuart. Your latest spate of e-mails leave me no choice.'

'Sexual harassment?'

'Yes.'

Purves growls: 'But we never even slept together.'

Noor looks away from his stare.

'Noorie. Noorie. You haven't a chance in hell of becoming a Law Partner in London if you go against me.'

He leaves.

She watches Kalandar in the distance cleaning up some mugs and walks over to him.

'Kalandar!'

He spins round and grins naturally.

'You've been avoiding me?'

He reflexively looks towards Nadeem's workstation.

She picks up his uncertainty, 'Please don't worry.'

He looks to the floor, so reminiscent of a child in trouble.

'I can see you have family issues here. No don't worry, I already know about Farah. I've done some research into your background. Nadeem's just jealous. Come on, it's

Friday tomorrow. Don't go home for the weekend. Why not come over to my apartment?'

'Er. I haven't seen all the important places in London. Yes, we could have a nice walk.'

'It's far too cold for a walk and you don't want to be seen by Nadeem or they'll send you back to Pakistan. Why not stay overnight? It does have two beds you know.'

She can see the confusion in his eyes.

'Er.'

She uncurls a strand of hair and notices him stare at her delicate hands.

'What excuse can I use? Uncle-ji Salman will be very suspicious.'

'I can fake some letters. They'll think you are on a weekend English language course run by the company.'

His heart is beating fast.

'Kalandar. It'll be fine. Do you want to spend time with me?'

'Er. No. Yes. No. I mean it would be great. To meet up. Can you really make it look as if I'm doing a course?'

'I'll have a bogus letter on company headed paper ready for you to present to your Uncle-ji later today. Don't forget to collect it from my office before you leave. It's all right. I'll send your cousin Nadeem on an errand. He won't see you pick it up. Inshallah.'

The
Guide,
Al-Hadi,
is He.
Events have
a patterning.
You may
find
chocolate
bars
growing in a
barren
desert and a
rising sun in
your bed at
night.

45

CHAPTER VI

Friday evening.

The expensive red Ferrari surprises Kalandar. The way Noor's long strands of jet-black hair curl mysteriously over her slender shoulders shocks him. He'd only seen such women on Bollywood billboards and never in real life. That the glamorous lady in red behind the wheel had asked *him* to be with her wasn't just unbelievable, it was... miraculous –surely this wasn't supposed to happen in this life.

He sits down and takes her easy smile in. Suddenly he's *very* cosy. Her hair begins to flutter as the car speeds out. In no time at all they are in her City Centre Apartment. Walls of glass surround him. She senses his thoughts.

'Kalandar don't worry, this is special glass – we can see outside. No one can see in.'

Noor kicks off her long heels and work dress. Kalandar looks away as she slips into comfy loungewear. She motions for him to sit with her at the leather couch.

He absorbs her aura. He is attracting swirls of baraka. His own subtle energies are solidifying. He's happy and relaxed. Everything around him is now more spiritually aware. *Returning to the world of archetypes.* A cushion of gluey baraka envelops his skin.

'Wow Kalandar there's so much heat coming off your body. It's amazing.' Her hands can sense the difference in him.

'Oh,' is the only thing he can say as his whole body feels her touch, even though she's not touching his physical body.

She continues to run her fingers a few centimetres away from his hands.

'This is where I feel more than heat,' her silky hennaed fingertips are at his palms.

'Can you perceive an invisible mist around me?'

'Yes!'

'Noor...'

'What is it?'

'I feel I'm going into another world when you run your fingers through my spirit body.'

'Your what?'

'Spirit body.'

'I didn't think we could feel the spirit in this world.'

'There are two blessings which deceive many people: health and free time.'

PROPHET
Muhammad
صلى الله عليه وسلم

Value His gifts of well-being and leisure. Fill your spare time with sunny sizzling love and be grateful for your health.

'Noor, you can see and feel anything you want. Allah has given this gift to us.'

Her mind becomes interested, 'You are so lucky to have lived in Pakistan. You must know everything there is to know about the Qur'an and the Prophet Muhammad peace be upon him.'

Kalandar's eyes blink suspiciously.

'What is it?'

'Nothing,' his enraptured eyes probe the bright lights of London against the black sky.

She gracefully stands up and pours him some juice in a heavy crystal glass.

He puts his highly energised hand in hers.

She notices his growing confidence.

Kalandar leads her to the main window.

She loves the feeling of him taking control. Makes her swoon. Can hear an Angelic Vocal Orchestra somewhere in the back of her mind.

Noor feels a gentle stroke at her hip where his fingers have deposited electric ripples. Waves of baraka cascade through her body. She clutches his strong frame for more support.

He whispers, 'Allah's earth is beautiful.'

'I've spent many long hours contemplating just that thought.'

The aroma of his musky breath astonishes her. Her head leans closer into his chest.

'This is perfection,' she whispers and holds him tight as rain begins to trickle down the glass.

'Can I ask you a question?'

'Of course.'

'Your heart says one thing but you do another.'

She looks sharply into his eyes, 'Do you mean Prince Freddie?'

She doesn't wait for him to answer: 'I foolishly have become involved in a relationship I don't want. Honestly Kalandar believe me. I'm in the process of ending it.'

'Your heart is warm. I have never felt anything but closeness from your blessed forehead.'

The sound of the Azaan breaks the spell.

Kalandar exhales gratefully at the sound of Islam here in rich opulent surroundings. *If this is a mirror of Paradise, then let me die today and enter jannah immediately. Or am I in heaven already?*

'Those who plant a tree or sow seeds from which humanity, animals or birds eat are rewarded until the Day of Rising.'

PROPHET Muhammad ﷺ

Pulsating love bears fruit in every season by the leave of Allah.

The bathroom was of marble. And the shower cubicle so huge that Kalandar mistook it for an extra room. The steam refreshed his soul and the black *Salwar Kameez* Noor had bought for him fit perfectly upon his slender lithe body.

As he stood on the prayer mat he sensed her glide next to him. She was clad from head to toe in a silky red Kameez-like gown.

He is aware of her presence as his forehead touches the ground. He is transported to another plane of existence during *sajda*. It is dark but illumined by a higher presence. Black light falls from her prayers to his left. He senses the Almighty Presence and her gentle symbols behind him.

Noor concentrates on each word of the Qur'an. As if her soul is holding a gigantic *tasbeeh* where each bead is an ayat of the Qur'an. She is cognisant of every Arabic stroke, meaning and each vowel and gentle inflection. She's reciting 'ihdinasiraatalmustaqim', concordantly her mind translates the Quranic Arabic *show us the straight path* – her thoughts flash everything - her emotions, fears and hopes. Towards a new future with the man praying by her side.

As they finish she giggles, 'Black and Red have always been my favourite. You're the black letters of the Qur'an and I'm the red dots.' She points to Islamic Calligraphy on the wall. An exquisite classical Arabic Piece of Art. Black and Red flowing like two lovers echoing Surah Yasin.

'It's late, what would you like to eat?' she switches on a voice activated Qur'an recitation. It is gentle, soft and soothingly cool. He follows her to the Persian style dining room. They sit on the floor on ornate cushions amidst the smell of lavender candles. The sweet melody of the Qur'an flavours their souls.

'Lavender was first distilled by Muslim scientists,' she says.

'I can see an angel being attracted to the smell.'

'Do you see the angel or do you feel him?'

Kalandar: 'I see him fluttering above in this room. Farishtay love nice smells.'

Noor: 'It's a hadith[22] you mean. The Prophet Muhammad. sal-Allaho, once said that Angels are attracted to pleasant fragrances.'

'I didn't mean a hadith – I meant, an angel.'

'Gosh. I never knew you could see angels, but wait..' she recalls another saying from memory, 'If you would consistently be good, then even angels would come and shake your hand. It's another hadith.'

'My Raani,' Kalandar smiles.

Noor's face turns golden in the ambient light of the candles and the baraka of the angel in harmony with the Qur'an.

He continues, 'My Raani, your head is full of great words.'

'Only words,' she silently observes. 'Whilst you see, I only read.'

'Nonsense, what you read, I can only see.'

She chuckles and hands him a menu, 'This is from the finest Panjaabi restaurant in London. We can order now and it will be delivered pretty sharply.'

He quickly speaks, 'I'll have Naan gosht please.'

'What sort of gosht?'

'Oh,' Kalandar looks at the menu, 'goat.'

She smiles, 'Order again. They don't do Halal Goat here.'

'Oh, Carella.'

'They don't do carella either.'

'Noor –I can't read.'

She feels his embarrassment, 'Like I said before, it's better to see rather than read.'

'You see, Abuji's business was doing so bad that he couldn't afford a good school.'

'Shhh. Please don't apologise. Didn't you know Prophet Muhammad *sal-Allaho,* couldn't read?'

'No I didn't.'

'Kalandar, do you know anything of our Nabi's life at all? Do you know any Surah of the Qur'an?'

He looks down, 'All I know is what I have seen in visions. Prophet Muhammad's smiling face, *sal-Allaho alayhi wa aleh hi wa salam*, and I've seen Angels guarding the Hidden Tablets. That's where the Heavenly Books are kept.'

'So what do you recite in Namaz?'

'I don't recite. I feel Him and pray to Him.'

'But will your Salaat be valid?'

His hands distressfully stroke his beard, 'Allah is the Most Forgiving. I think it doesn't matter what I recite. It's what goes on in your heart. Words are only supposed to get you close to Allah. Most people confuse the Qur'an with Allah nowadays. Allah isn't the Qur'an.'

'You don't understand me. I don't confuse Allah with the Qur'an.'

'The best of you are those who are the best to their women.'

PROPHET Muhammad صلى الله عليه وسلم

Those who are smitten with the Divine are amiable in every exchange.

'Then why do you concentrate on what each word sounds like and what each word means instead of praying to Allah.'

'It *is* praying to Allah.'

'But don't you spend too much time reading rather than feeling?'

'You have a point Kalandar. You're making me think! Perhaps I'm too book-orientated. I saw you looking at the statue of Buddha at the entrance. I don't pray to Buddha. It just helps me unwind. I do yoga for inner peace.'

'I get it through Namaz.'

'Uh. How I wish I could reach that level of Ibadat through Islam.'

'I'm sorry Noor, I'm being horrible to you. What gives me the right to question you when you read the Mysterious Qur'an? I can learn a lot from you. I've always wanted to read it.'

'Don't apologise. You are passionate about Allah. I can see that. Now how about ordering some food?'

Kalandar: 'I'm not hungry I think I'll go to sleep. Need to get up for Salaat-e-Fajr.'

His eyes flick instinctively towards her bedroom.

'Good idea. I wake up early too. Kalandar?'

'Ji?'

'Would you please do the Azaan for me in the morning. I'd love to hear it from your lips, uh could we pray together?'

'Of course.'

His bedroom's huge. Roomy and pearl-white, leading to another marble en suite. Noor had taken the trouble to order a Satin *Kurta Pyjama* for his nightwear. He decides to shower and then lies down nervously on the enormous bed. Can hear light movements from her room.

He thinks she's knocking on his door. His heart flutters. Faints, luckily for him, on the bed.

'Kalandar?'

He vaguely makes out the beginnings of dawn. Seems like no time has passed.

'You slept very soundly. Sorry I came into your room. I just wanted to wake you for Fajr.'

'Already?'

'Don't worry. If you're tired you can snooze for a little while longer.'

They pray in silence and they are soon outside. She spots a continental-style eatery. They sit down for breakfast.

She orders a passion fruit smoothie.

'This world is enjoyment, and the best of its enjoyment is a righteous woman.'

PROPHET Muhammad ﷺ

Pleasure is part of the Creator's Wonder.

'No lassie or paratha?' Kalandar pretends to read the menu.

'No goat either,' smiles Noor.

She yawns, 'Couldn't sleep last night.' Her face flashes him a mischievous grin.

He tries to see if they sell rusk cakes. Smiles, 'It was all too much for me. I think I fainted.'

'What will you have?' she asks pleasantly.

'Your lips.'

'Uh. Kalandar?'

'Sorry, I meant...'

Their conversation is broken by the rattle of plates.

Breakfast finishes in a happy silence, as they are about to leave Kalandar pushes a five-pound note into the hands of the manager, who looks at him blankly. Noor smiles and adds a twenty-pound note to his.

'I could have bought a whole roast leg of goat for that much in Pakistan,' he says to Noor before sinking into a shameful disposition.

She tugs him close to her, fills up the Ferrari and soon they're roaring along the motorway, instrumental sitar and tabla filling the air around them.

'Where are we going?'

Noor: 'Want to go anywhere special?'

'The sea. I've heard England is surrounded by oceans.'

'Hmm, it's not exactly Barbados, Kalandar.'

'Baba who?'

She laughs. 'I mean England isn't really sun-shiningly great on coasts. Blustery yes.'

'Or somewhere green?'

'Green, hmm,' she opens the glove compartment and throws a red rose into the lap of a bashful Kalandar.

She comes off the motorway at the first brown tourist sign.

They reach a majestic looking old ivy-ridden Historic House enclosed by gardens.

Kalandar thankfully kicks away his shoes, walks on the cut grass, far from the path. Noor leans on him to abandon her own boots. The green fields seem to come alive under their feet.

He looks up into the blue sky and then into the brown sky of Noor's eyes. He longs to stroke her face but refrains. Diverts his attention downwards, only to stop at her bare

'If I were to command anyone to prostrate to anyone else, I would have commanded women to prostrate to their husbands.'

PROPHET Muhammad ﷺ

An apparent rank of the vernacular lover towards the Beloved is that of Creature /Creator. But Reality is such that adoration is to the Supreme Being. Allah Unlimited.

feet. Reflexively turns to the horizon and feels the Love of Allah. He chuckles.

'What is it Kalandar?'

'There is so much beauty that I don't know where to look!'

'You can look into me. Let me be your comfort in moments of uncertainty.'

He breathes deeply and stares straight into her soul. Her eyes vanish and he takes in her essence.

Dizzily she drops to the ground and he picks her up. Her lips are ever so close to his.

His unquenchable thirst crawls along his bodily hair and ends up in the moonlight of her dazzling eyes. No physical kiss, yet both lips seem to taste each other as if they are soaring in heavenly embrace.

Every drop of her is drunk in that moment. Yet their bodies haven't made contact. Her smooth skin senses every fibre of his warm movement. She is flying amongst the stars and for the first time in her life perceives a new, though familiar, warmth. Is this shadow a prelude to the Majestic Love of Allah?

Silence.

Drowned in each other, the confused pair manage to stagger towards a great oak. The bewildered two lean against the heavily rooted tree

Kalandar looks up, 'We've crossed the threshold of the human world.'

'What do you mean?'

'Half close your eyes,' he whispers in Urdu.

She does so and views the changing colour of the sky. It turns purple and the tree becomes icy white. Kalandar's face becomes jetblack. His hair a fiery red.

Her own hands turn red and her tresses become strands of pure glistening gold. She stares into his piercingly bright starry eyes, as she does so, it's as if her tongue is tasting him. She touches his hands for comfort and senses the entire galaxy joining with her. 'Kalandar!'

'Sssh,' his gentle hands comb her hair and as her strands become undone, the sky falls down into her lips. His face replaces it and in his eye she makes out the silhouette of the Taj Mahal. Black.

An Angel covers the entrance and a Mughal-like Prince stands holding a diamond crown bearing the name 'Noor'. She blinks and realises that it's not a Mughal Prince.

It's Kalandar.

Your environment is not what it seems.
The grass of your interpretation should
be forever green.

53

CHAPTER VII

They are accelerating back into London. It's freezingly, almost diabolically cold, yet the car's top is down and the raw wind is blowing onto their excited faces.

'Kalandar, never in my wildest dreams would I have hoped to experience what we did! Wow!'

Kalandar is tucking into an ice-cream, enjoying the moment: A beautiful girl, fast Ferrari and of course, the Visions given by Allah. What else does a man need?

She asks him to open the glove compartment.

He opens the package and finds a silver plated mobile phone.

'For you. Everyone has a mobile and so should you. It also means we can talk whenever we want to. The bills come to my address, so don't worry!'

He pretends to speak into the phone like a businessman closing a Trillion Rupee deal. She laughs at his boyish antics:

'The evening is young, eh Kalandar? Would you like to go to a restaurant for roti or come back to my place and we can snuggle up to a movie or just talk?'

Her excited self is momentarily distracted by her own phone, ringing on her hands free.

He watches her white teeth glisten in the awakening flickering motorway lights.

Then the unexpected happens.

Her smile fades, lips curling in a new tension.

'Oh Allah. I should be at the airport. Prince Freddie is waiting! Oh my Allah, how could I have forgot? Our plane leaves in just under two hours. We were supposed to be going to Agra tonight, stay a few hours and come back tomorrow!'

'What, I thought you and Freddie had finished.'

'Finished? Kalandar, I can't let him down like this! I *will* end the relationship with him soon. I'll tell him in Agra.'

His attempts to understand her thoughts only meet her undecipherable eyes.

Silence.

Deafening silence.

She punches a new destination on her sat-nav. 'If I hurry, I could still get there in time.'

He feels as if he's not there. That she has detached herself from him.

Not another word is spoken until the car stops at its destination. Royal plain clothes security officials whisk Noor away.

As she's leaving him she whispers, 'Kalandar I'm so sorry. Please do understand, I promised Freddie I'd be there for his trip to India. I'll ask the Prince's men to take you home. I can't hug you goodbye - there could be paparazzi here. Can't tell you how sorry I am. I'll only be gone for a short while. I'll be back at my desk on Monday inshallah. I'll make it up to you I promise.'

He watches her go.

Then his feelings get the better of him. His easily provoked irascible complex has been awakened. *How could Noor do such a thing? Go off like this? First she invites him, says she has no feelings for the Crown Prince, then decides to ditch him here.*

He runs. And runs. And runs.

This is why he never learnt to read. Emotionally he can't control himself. Good or bad. He screams and crazily darts off into the dark night.

Noor sits beside the Prince. A corner of her heart feels a sudden pain.

'Oh darling, you missed a most scrumptious supper!' Prince Freddie himself starts to strap Noor into her seat.

'You are looking so very elegant my dear. But why so charmingly quiet?'

Thoughts rain inside her. *What on earth am I doing here? How could I have left my Kalandar? Why did I do it? What's wrong with me? Surely I could have just told Freddie on the phone that I couldn't come with him. Am I too impressed by Royalty? How is Kalandar? My Allah, what have I done?*

In vain she looks out to see if she can see him. But there is nothing to see. Only darkness of the night, as their plane heads towards India.

* * *

Kalandar wakes up and finds himself on a park bench. Briskly dusts himself down. *Oh Allah please take me back*

'Part of what I fear for you after I have gone is the beauty and attraction of this world, which will be opened up to you.'

PROPHET
Muhammad صلى الله عليه وسلم

Your beloved's beauty is an *ishara*. An indication of the seductive beauty of the awaited garden in Paradise.

'This world is the prison of the believer and the paradise of the unbeliever.'

PROPHET Muhammad

Remain in the jail of enamoured love. Your needs are few and your moments together with your beloved sparse: for you are in the service of humankind. This world is a prison as Actual Love can only happen in the spirit – one can only take and give love fully in the hereafter. Lovers long to leave this abode and discover the garden of forever.

to the Panjaab. This isn't how I thought life would be in England. Not what Shaykh Junoon prophecised. Is he just a village pir, a nonsensical mendicant?

He's still wearing the Black Salwaar Kameez Noor had given him. About to take it off and then has a recollection of Noor's sympathetic forehead. He strokes the luxurious fabric. He's both tense and relaxed. Angry and content. Vehemently riled at her sudden exit, yet desirous for her and anxious to be in the intimate caress of her company.

He can see the golden dome of a Mosque. Startled, he moves closer. 'What's a Mosque doing here in a London park?'

He walks on the carpet looking for a place to pray. Somewhere near the front.

Inexplicably, as he looks up at the *Mihrab*, a Qur'anic verse instantly pops into his head. He casts his eyes at it again. It's writing. *He can now read!* He looks at the writing on the wooden pillars and takes in the 99 Names of Allah. It feels as if the puzzle of the written world has left him.

Shakily he looks around him at the carpeted universe of the Mosque and then reads the time for the next Jam'aa. *What is happening to me?*

* * *

Freddie looks out of the hotel veranda. The lazy Indian sun begins to climb for another day, 'Oh I get it. You don't like India? Dearest, you almost chide my soul with your unhappy disposition. What is it? Why your beguiling eyes so red and tearful?'

Noor stretches and yawns, 'I'm just tired. I don't hate India.'

Prince Freddie: 'I've ordered the PM to explain why he is sending more troops to Pakistan. If you ask me, he's creating another Afghanistan, the dastardly devil. My charity is doing all it can. Pfah! Politicians. They care nothing for the unfortunate poor. Down with Parliament and their damned MPs if you ask me!'

'It's nice of you to support common people – they are innocent.'

'I know darling. Aaah. Great things! Our conveyance has arrived.'

She makes pleasant conversation on the way.

The Taj Mahal.

Pure white marble.

It's the incredible picturesque outline that grabs her. Doesn't even seem as if it's of this earth. Just like the movies. Madly Romantic.

She gazes at the pond, the reflection perhaps representing the mysterious Heavenly Jannah. *The Promised Garden of Al-Qur'an.*

'Isn't this a fruitful way to spend one's time?'

She nods, watching the birds and thinking of Nana Abu-ji and how much she missed her family. At home she wasn't treated like royalty, but it was far more meaningful.

'Oh, did I forget to mention? A desperate Professor of Mughal History from Delhi wanted to have a private word with you. Odd old fellow, but thoroughly ravishing.'

Professor Irfan Masud is wearing a cream coloured pyjama suit. His hair is short and his beard has no moustache. Noor instantly recognises it as a gesture of piety as is the dark mark of prayer on his crumpled forehead.

He seems to have an urgent message and takes her to one side, speaking in Urdu.

'Hai Raani aa gae ho? Salam alaikum Princess!'

'Wa alaikum as-salam, but I'm not a Princess.'

'Oh but you are. I've researched your family history.'

'How could you have done?'

'I'm Mughal blood myself. We are related.'

She doesn't know what to say. He continues, 'My dear the continuation of the Mughal Empire lies with you.'

'What are you saying?'

'By marrying Prince Frederick you'll reclaim past glory. You must find out all you can about Muslim Mughal rule and then bring Musalmaan Rule to England. It is only from afar that peace can be brought to this region.'

'What?'

'Our hope of a resurgent Mughal Empire lies with you. You're the one to introduce the Mahal and Musalmaan culture into Europe. This is your destiny. Please understand

'In the evening, do not anticipate the morning, and in the morning do not anticipate the evening.'

PROPHET Muhammad

In the moment of zealous love, fully breathe the crazy flashy instance before it goes.

me. I've no time to explain. Perhaps when you get back to England I'll e-mail. Your Nana-Abu and me are friends. We were spies. We fought against Imperialism and the corrupt Maharaja Princes. We hid our involvement.'

'Nana-Abu is no spy. He never fought in any war. He's a wonderful man of letters!'

'Please believe me. Has he never told you of our glorious past?'

'He hasn't mentioned you nor any involvement in espionage. He can't even tie his own shoe lace!'

Professor Irfan is agitated, 'Child listen. Of course he can't speak secrets to you. The Mughals! Has he told you of our ancestry? Surely he's passed on this knowledge down to you? About the Mughals!'

'Look, I'm confused. I've just got off a plane and my head is dizzy. Prince Freddie will be wanting me to sit with him for dinner. Then we fly back. And you - a complete stranger pop up and tell me about my Nana-Abu.'

He looks at her. Pauses. Then excitedly speaks in English, without stopping to pause for a breath, his Indian accent getting deeper as he does, 'Noor. Allah brought you hear for a purpose! My gosh look at you! You even look like a Mughal. You talk like a Mughal. Everything about you. No wonder Prince Freddie is in love with you. But I'm not stupid. I wasn't born yesterday – I can see you don't love him at all. Which is a shame – you can save Pakistan from war and thousands, nay, millions of lives could be saved if you marry him. A Muslim Queen of England. That's what we need. You don't have to love a man to marry him. My own marriage was arranged and I'm happy.'

A Security Guard comes in between the two: 'Noor, the Prince kindly requests your presence.'

She continues to question the spectacled gaze of the Professor. 'Give me your e-mail,' she says, 'I'll contact you inshallah.'

* * *

Uncle-ji Salman has just dropped off a passenger at the Mosque. Decides to park up and pray. After all, it's almost prayer time and it is a *khubsoorat Masjid*. He respectfully enters the main hall, irritated, he rubs his moustache as he can't find any *topis*. *Must be an Arab place, don't they have any ikhtiraam at all? Keeping their heads uncovered?*

'The most truthful phrase ever said by a poet is the words of Labid: *Everything except Allah is false.'*

PROPHET Muhammad

Ecstatic Love is a shadow. It isn't existent of itself. So where is it coming from? The perception of love, when we feel it, is a whizzing train. Destination: Allah!

He sees a man trembling in the middle of the hall.

'Buffoon. What an idiot showing himself up in the *Maseet* of all places. Bloody ulu ka patha,' he thinks to himself.

Then realises:

It's Kalandar.

'Owaaay!' Uncle-ji Salman forgets he's in the Mosque. His shout is heard by all.

Kalandar recognises his Uncle.

'Chacha-ji? Aaap yaha kiya kar rahae ho?'

'I should be asking that question young man. Shouldn't you be on a language course?

'I got lost.'

After prayers, he takes him home. He's still officially at work, so drives off, leaving Auntie-ji and Kalandar alone with Farah.

'Farah dear, haven't you got work to do upstairs?'

'No,' she firmly says through a mouthful of pizza, 'can't you see I'm watchin the telly?'

Auntie-ji smiles to Kalandar. She offers him a pizza slice, 'How was your English course?'

Kalandar is bad at lying, 'The course was really good. Acha tha.'

She asks, 'Angrayzie aa gai hae?'

'I can now read,' Kalandar replies honestly.

* * *

As the plane is beginning it's ascent, Noor can feel her pulsating heart surrounded by a Greater Entity than herself. A Divine Presence. And it feels so real. As if she is almost touching *The Sacred Source*. Normally she'd recite a prayer for travel, but today it's not coming to her mind. Yet she can vividly perceive Allah's protection and the anchor of her soul is at peace.

Prince Freddie: 'Wow, that lunch was a bit heavy. My ruddy tongue is famished for a liquid though. How about a light drink. I'll of course have the ready Champagne. What juice would you fancy? We could ask that rather nicely turned out new airhost for drinks.'

As the drinks list is placed in front of her, she blinks and screams out in horror:

'I can't read!'

'Pardon dearest?'

'None of you eats better food than that which he eats as a result of the work of his own hand.'

PROPHET
Muhammad

Give your beloved the produce of your labour. Nothing borrowed, nothing acquired. Bring all of you to bear upon your Soul-Mirror.

'Be in this world as if you were a stranger or a traveller on the road.'

PROPHET Muhammad

Love is in no need of Palace chambers. That sweet love is whole where there are no ties to the world's fixtures and fittings. Love with the awareness that this life is fleeting and your attachment is to an exciting Hereafter. A tantalising soul world described in the Qur'an.

'The letters. They just look like blobs,' she looks around her in horror, 'and the words on the wall look like incomprehensible symbols.'

'Hmmm. It's all seemed Greek to me anyway. I'll call my Physician. Please don't panic, you're not used to travelling.'

'I'm not ill,' she sobs as he holds her hand, 'what's happening to me?'

* * *

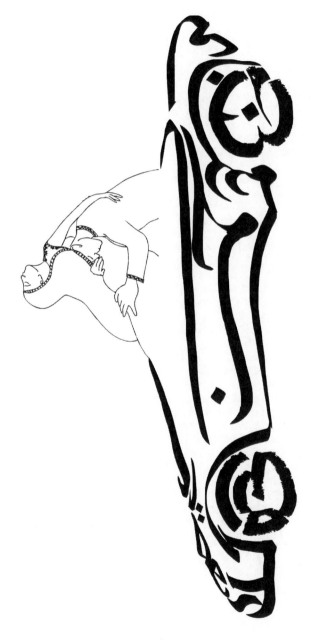

This world is a vehicle given shape through the Creative construction of Allah. Read the words behind each form. Love and attachment of this abode is upon the wheels of *Bismillah.* Park your love in His Fortress.

61

'It is a right of Allah that nothing elevates itself in this world, without Him then bringing it low.'

PROPHET Muhammad

Position and status in this world changes –

unbroken love doesn't. As loyal love, being Sacred, belongs to another Realm.

CHAPTER VIII

Monday morning and all isn't well. Kalandar is struggling to come to terms with the rude abruptness Noor left him 'stranded' in London. And Noor? Well, she struggled to read the briefing papers for her morning Client and has an important meeting at 11am with the Unions too. On top of that she's feeling really guilty about Kalandar. And just to make things more complicated, Prince Freddie is going to Bradford as well. Later in the week. Friday night, to be precise.

The London streets seem freezing compared to the Panjaab.

Noor is gloomily walking away from the Client's office.

'Why didn't you read your case notes this morning?' Purves says, looking down her shirt.

'How could you tell I hadn't?'

'Obvious. Too obvious.'

'I was busy Stuart.'

'Yes I heard. It was on the news. You and Freddie were basking in India. I do hope you have your wits about you when you defend your own job here later on.'

She's exhausted and falls asleep in her chair.

Purves is happy not to wake her for her eleven o'clock meeting. This will show her inefficiency to Personnel. As he is putting a large *'Do not Disturb'* sign on her door, he gasps at the sight of her sleeping body. Twitches his trouser zipper. Then shuts the door.

Kalandar's shift is about to start. He peers round the corner and sees the sign on her office, *so that's her new ploy to avoid me. She doesn't want to talk to me today.* He looks down at his mop and bucket. Then his reflection in a computer monitor screen causes him to freeze in mid-stride. *I shouldn't really blame her. Look at me compared to a Prince. I'm a toilet cleaner and don't look like a Bollywood hero. Freddie is gora, wealthy and can take her to the Taj Mahal and back in one weekend. Whilst all I can do is carry her there in spirit only, and even then, the Taj Mahal was Black.*

Dejectedly walks into the toilet and bumps into his supervisor, 'You! Go back and clean the female loo again. Thaek hai?'

'I cleaned it this morning.'

'There's loads of urine and shit underneath the toilets. You haven't cleaned the ttati from beneath the rims either. I can smell it from here. Taro bahp tareli ttati khayee! Do it now. Thaek hai?'

He pushes his trolley into the Ladies and hangs up the 'Male Cleaner' sign.

As he is cleaning, he encounters a sweet, rather than a nasty aroma - and is soon face to face with a weary Noor.

'Are you OK?' Kalandar forgets all about his own troubles with her.

'I'm fine. Just missed one important meeting. Had an awful meeting earlier. I feel so sorry about Saturday evening.'

Kalandar's heart almost breaks at her state, 'Can I get you some water?'

'Please,' she falls on his shoulder.

'Noor...'

'Oh. Sorry!' she pulls herself together. 'I'm putting us both at risk. There might be someone around.'

'No. Only you seem to ignore the 'Male Cleaner' signs.'

'Oh. Is that what the sign said. Kalandar, I can't read anymore.'

'Noor, isn't that odd. I can read now. I don't know how it's happened, but I *can* read.'

They both freeze.

He helps her back to her feet and whispers, 'Go to your office. I'll be there shortly.'

He brings in a cup of water. She sees him put his hand over it.

'What are you doing?'

'I'm sending baraka into the drink so that you can be cured.'

She gratefully gulps it down.

'Oh, I'll get some soup for you. It's normally you who orders lunches for me!'

She giggles.

Noor takes the hot steaming cup and sips it slowly, 'Thank you for blessing the water for me earlier, but I still can't comprehend the written word. How could we have swapped places?'

'Allah has revealed that you should be humble so no one should vaunt himself above another, and none should commit injustice against another.'

PROPHET
Muhammad

The tide of fizzy love covers all upon the shore with equal degrees of fondness.

'Shall I tell you about the people of the Fire? All those who are coarse, dominating and arrogant.'

PROPHET Muhammad

Temper your soul with the mallet of golden love. Blue watered love has maximum power to soften hearts.

'I don't know. Somehow we've penetrated each other's spirit and taken bits from each other.'

'Kalandar, I'm so happy that you can unravel script, but if I can't read I'll have to give up my job, my business and everything.'

He notices her trembling lips. She seems so vulnerable.

'Well, if I was to give your skills back to you?'

'How? The brain's processing centres aren't child's play. We'll need a neuro-scientist to help us.'

'What are you talking about? It's not the brain that's done it. It's our souls that have dangerously criss-crossed.'

She pushes her hand in his and whispers:

'How do we uncross them?'

Kalandar's eyes talk to hers.

She realises what he means. Pushes a chair against the already locked door. Draws the blinds.

In the dark office, he puts his hands in hers. She is aware of baraka surges between them.

A light shines from his forehead and she feels her own head being massaged by that light. She blinks. Blue rain is falling around them. A dark green moon in the distance casts a turquoise sheen to the moment. She doesn't want to be anywhere else and happily loses everything that's familiar to her. He's falling towards her. Love is brightly freshening the newness of the interplay. Change. Transformation. His being merges into her heart and plucks all the graves of *dunyavi* earth out. There is *mmmmmmmmmmmmm*. Goodness. Reasons why a breeze moves and how an apple falls to the ground. Higher beats are filling her as a crescendo is blazing on each of her fingers. Anticipating the final surge, she considers the alien affection of one other than her own. A vocabulary enters the soul and shoots peace into her mind.

She awakens in her couch and finds Kalandar lying unconscious on the floor of her office. She touches his chest and he comes to.

Sits him on the chair.

Then she looks for no reason at all towards the empty cup lying on the floor.

Kalandar still seems to be in a daze, so she suggests:

'No water here, I'll get you another drink from the fountain.'

She's not exactly in a state to walk but opens her office door. Sees odd beings walking and floating whilst her colleagues work at their desks.

Frightened. She shuts the door.

Then looks up to the ceiling. Takes a few deep breaths. Touches the furniture of her office. Grabs familiar objects.

'Bismillah irRahman irRaheem,' opens the door again.

Back to normal.

Walks with her hands grabbing the walls. She needs something solid to keep her earthed.

She returns. A fully awake Kalandar greets her.

His benevolent gaze falls on the dust of her soul.

She sits and looks out of the window. Tears running down both her cheeks.

Turning to Kalandar, 'Are you well? I think you collapsed.'

'I saw wonderful things.'

'So did I.'

'You're crying.'

'I can read again.'

'But why are you crying?'

Noor: 'I felt your deep grief and anger at what I did to you on Saturday.'

'Didn't you also feel the euphoria you give me too?'

'I felt how sorry you feel for yourself and that makes me sad.'

Kalandar: 'Some might say we now know each others thoughts.'

'Others would say we have become each other.'

In their disorientated state, they don't notice Nadeem, who has been observing them through a space in the blinds.

***

Kalandar is reliving today's memories in his attic bedroom when Farah and Nadeem enter without knocking.

'You are a real Casanova aren't you?' Nadeem shows him the fuzzy video of Noor and him in the office that he's taken on his mobile phone. Nadeem says nothing. And shows no emotion.

Farah: 'I never did want to marry you. Now I've got the perfect excuse not to.'

'The worst of people in the sight of Allah on the Day of Rising is a man who goes to his wife or his wife goes to him and then they disclose their secrets to others.'

PROPHET Muhammad

Ardent love blends with Secrecy. That which remains private, untold and unravelled is that which stands upon Holy ground.

'Are you going to send me to Pakistan?'

Nadeem is still in his work clothes, he gently loosens the gold cufflink on his left wrist, 'There are no Airlines prepared to go there since the war started.'

Farah interrupts: 'Me and my boyfriend have been waiting for this moment. I want to marry Fiaz. Someone whom I love, and who loves me.'

Kalandar: 'H-have you told Uncle-ji or Auntie?'

Nadeem looks at him with disgust, 'What do you take us for. Do you think we're goray? We love our parents. They would be devastated if they found out what you were doing. Ham ko bae sharam karna hae? Aap ko koi izzat-behsty ka nahi pata? There are just two things we'd like you do: firstly, after marrying Farah, move out of our house. You will never sleep with Farah nor live with her. You will pretend that you have a job abroad and we will never need to see your two-timing face again. You'll also send maintenance to Farah and allow my sister to see who she wants.'

'And the second thing?'

'Second 'thing' is this: Once you are out of our house you will never, and I mean *never* talk to our parents ever. They have been so kind to you, how could you have let us down like this.'

Kalandar is angry too: 'Didn't you think of my feelings when you knew full well that Farah was already seeing someone else?'

'Nothing is sacred in England,' Nadeem sneers remarkably well for a man with education.

Kalandar shakes his head: 'No. It's not that. To you I'm just a *mangaytar* – someone who you think is desperate to be in England. You don't believe I have feelings, dreams and aspirations. You see all those who live in Pakistan as scroungers. We come here and become imprisoned by our own extended family. I heard all the stories in Lahore and never believed them. What makes you better than me? It doesn't matter, there's no justice in your heart despite you having studied it.'

'I didn't say I was better than you. But remember that you clean the toilets and I use them.'

'Nadeem, my cousin, please think what you are saying. Just because you have gone to school here and can speak English like an Englishman it doesn't mean you are better

'Anyone who believes in Allah and the Last Day should honour guests.'

PROPHET Muhammad

People who you receive are guests. Allow comforting love to shine from your eyes to comfort and console humanity's wandering lost souls.

than a man from Pakistan. It's what's in here that counts,'
Kalandar punches his chest.

'And what is in your heart? Noor? Don't lecture me on
rights and wrongs of migration.'

Angry Kalandar: 'This is the reason you want rid of me.
You can't handle the fact that despite you having a
university degree and perfected westernised manners, you
didn't win her love but an uneducated me-no-English took
your heart's desire away.'

Farah intervenes with unexpected and for her, amazing
maturity: 'We've said what we wanted to say. Now shut it
the both of you. I can hear Ami-ji calling you. Khana tyar ho
ga.'

* * *

Noor is lying in bed. Her head aches after having surfed
the net on science, Islam and metaphysics. Still no answer
to what has happened between her and Kalandar.

As she is contemplating washing her hair, the intercom
buzzes.

'Who is it?'

A lively voice answers: 'Ameena!'

Noor: 'What on earth?'

'Nana Abu-ji insisted we keep our visit a secret.'

'I've buzzed you in. Come on up. Let me order you guys a
meal I've nothing cooked.'

'We've bought some of Ami-ji's pillau for you.'

They slump on the sofa and Noor begins to tell them off
for taking two trains and a taxi when she could have
arranged for a more comfortable mode of transport.

Nana-Abu: 'My baytti! Can we talk in private?'

They leave Ameena to watch a Bollywood music channel.
And anyway, she feels happier watching music videos alone.

The old man takes with him a cup of masala cha that Noor
insisted on making.

Noor's fatigued face is disturbing Nana-ji: 'Raanie, I've
got some important things to say but if you are tired then it
can wait until morning.'

'I won't be able to sleep.'

'I've come especially in person as I have really crucial
things to talk about. I also heard about you looking very
exhausted from my dear friend Professor-ji. Remember you
met him?'

'Anyone who believes in Allah and the Last Day, should maintain ties of kinship.'

PROPHET Muhammad

There are many facets to faithful love. Indeed, to nurture closeness of blood relationships has a connection with the prism of selflessness.

'Anyone who believes in Allah and the Last Day, should speak well or be silent.'

PROPHET Muhammad صَلَّى اللهُ عَلَيْهِ وَسَلَّم

So why talk negatively? Don't think badly. Feel good and speak it loud. If the world is too much, find a quiet spot and remain silent in prayer and Muraqbah. Release yourself from spoiling babble. Throw commotion into bins for the politicians to rummage through.

'Yes, only this weekend in Delhi. I had no idea you were once a spy! You guys are unbelievable.'

'We may look like *budday*, but believe me, we are young at heart. I'm going to stay and cook for you, look after you. And we can go back together on Thursday night. You need someone close to you.'

'I'm happy alone. But it's so nice of you to think about me. Nana-ji, you know that the spare room was meant for you. Please do stay. But what are the important things you want to talk to me about?'

'It's about Prince Frederick and him coming to Bradford on Juma day. You're too young to see the importance of this on world affairs.'

'You mean Pakistan?'

'Not only Pakistan, but all the other Muslim countries that are at conflict with the West. Britain is still important in global politics. If you were Queen, you could influence the course of history.'

'I can influence Prince Freddie as a friend.'

'He would listen to a wife much more.'

'But Nana-ji, I don't love him.'

'My child. It pains me to say this, you are my favourite grandchild, but you will have to forego love for the reshaping of humanity. We Mughals have always had to put love second. Only Emperor Shah Jehan put the love of his life before the affairs of state.'

'And look what happened – he built the Taj Mahal.'

'Behty!! O meri sonniyeh! Aurangzayb, his own son, ended up imprisoning Shah Jehan at home as his love had turned into near-lunacy.'

'So the Black Taj Mahal was never built? As he was not allowed to show his full love?'

'That may be the case, but ironically a universal truth was revealed in its non-completion.'

'Respected Nana-ji please explain what you mean.'

'The Love that's imprisoned in the heart is far more enjoyable than love that is spoilt by physical encounter – a love in the *ruh*, in the *dil*, is the love that has no limits.'

'Love is in a Taj Mahal of the heart? Is that where ultimate reality is? I see many things in that other inner world. I see visions and they seem real to me. In one such a vision I saw a Black Taj Mahal. It felt grander and more magnificent than even the so-called real Taj Mahal in Agra.'

Nana-Abu-ji is in tears, 'I saw it too. The Black Taj Mahal in a dream. And I saw him there as you must have.'

'Saw whom?'

In a show of Eastern embarrassment, the aged *bazurg* lowers his head, 'Him. The one whom you desire. A wandering beggar from Pakistan...'

She puts her hand on his shoulder and whispers, 'He is no beggar. He is the most wonderful man I have ever met.'

He turns his head slowly towards her: 'You are right about him not being a beggar by lineage. He's a descendant of the Lodhi Sultans. Their Delhi Sultanate ruled over the Panjaab for a short time before our great ancestor Babar put an end to them. I believe he is named Kalandar.'

'How do you know so much about him? How did you manage to describe him and even know his name by a dream?'

'Dreams can uncover truths Noor.'

She sighs and senses the pain in his mind. Begins to massage his scalp. She can see more tears in his eyes.

'Noor, all I wanted for you is a simple life without worry. But you are the one remaining Mughal Princess in the world who could rule again. Promise me you'll think about what I've said.'

'Will I really be able to stop war between Muslims and the Western world?'

'If you follow *Qismat* yes. And my dear, you would never have any difficulty in bringing the light of Islam here once you are a Princess.'

She can see the logic. No more rushed 9am until late work commitments and a chance to save the world. But on the other side of the balance: the mysteries of the universe and –Kalandar. It's such a finely balanced equation.

Nana-Abu chortles to himself.

'What is it?'

'Do you know why I've brought little Ameena along with me?'

'To help you catch the right trains?'

'Good heavens no. To make the atmosphere more like home. We've had enough talk for now. Come on let's relax. There's a really nice take-away in London I don't often go to. It's cheap, not really fitting for a Princess, but the khana is first class. Not at all like Karachi.'

Noor hugs him, 'Do you know? My Nana-Abu-ji is,' and she adds a Panjaabi accent, 'very first class.'

'Part of what people know of the words of the first prophethood is that if someone is not shy, he can do whatever he likes.'

PROPHET Muhammad
صلى الله عليه وسلم

The reason love has lost much of its mystery, is that shame and coyness has been removed from today. Having a childhood innocence doesn't mean losing your confidence or exploring. Oh OK... be confident, but have a conscience.

* * *

Kalandar rings her mobile number.
Her summery voice: 'I'm having food with my family.'
'Oh. Sorry. I didn't know you were in Bradford.'
'I'm not. I'm at a place called *Chicken Burger Hi Burger*.'
'Kiya? The Burgerrie? Some people say that's the best *o'tal* in London. It's not far from where I live. I can walk to you inshallah.'
'No. You can't! My Nana Abu-ji and choti bayn are with me.'
'Oh.'
'Kalandar?'
'Ji?'
'You sound so different when you whisper on the phone.'
Kalandar: 'So do you. It makes me tingle.'
'Ji. Sorry! I can't talk now. I better get back to the table. I'll ring you later.'
'Inshallah.'
'Inshallah. Allah Hafez.'

* * *

Kalandar has been watching the phone under the covers for hours. It's switched on silent but at the first hint of a vibration he immediately grabs it and puts it close to his ear.
'Salam alaikum.'
'Wa alaikum salam.'
'Everyone is sleeping. Look I've been doing some research on the Net about what's happening to us.'
Kalandar, 'You mean, when we get close together?'
'Ha ji! The Qur'an says that a male and female were originally one soul. Well, my interpretation is that we were once *one* being, then Allah split us and made us a *pair*. But when we get together we return to our original state. There's more: In Quantum physics there is such a thing as synchronicity and an underlying field of Unity. It means that everything is all connected. So when we feel sympathetic to each other we become one person again.'
'Sympathetic?'
'Oh. It means when we feel deeply for one another.'
'Why can't you just say the word *love*?'

'Man should not use water left over by woman and neither the woman use water left over by the man. Rather they should both take a handful together.'

PROPHET
Muhammad
ﷺ

There are courtesies and manners in the avenue of affection.

Noor suddenly stops.

Kalandar: 'Sorry. I should not have used the word love.'

Noor: 'Kalandar, what words can I use to describe the confusion in my mind right now.'

'Is it about love?'

'It's about what this world wants out of me and what I want from this world. They are two opposing juggernauts that one day may crash and cause the one I cherish the most to get hurt the most.'

'I'm not following you.'

'I have to talk to you about Prince Freddie.'

'Again!'

'It's not what you're thinking. It's about what's happening in Pakistan and to the Muslims the world over. I may be forced to marry him to save many people from dying.'

She agonises for a while, then, 'I do love you. But I cannot say it. Nor do I think can we consummate our love.'

Kalandar pulls the covers over his head and asks Allah for a way out.

Noor: 'Please don't think I'm happy or content with any of this. You are the only man, actually, only one, who has ever made me feel whole.'

'Whatever Allah decides is always of a symbol of His Rehmat,' Kalandar says as his Sufi self talks to him.

'Hang on,' Noor's words are hardly perceptible.

A lull.

He waits an age.

'Oh, I think Ameena is at the door. I need to switch off for now,' Noor goes to see what she wants.

The news knocks Kalandar unconscious. His soul burns then disappears into a cloud. He tastes black ink running through his veins. Then turns totally pure black. And sees a red hue in the distance. Recognises it as Noor's red soul. He sinks in the ocean of pearl-water and discovers a rising cloud. In that moment a Divine Symphony of Angels assemble before him:

The redness of her body reveals itself and he says:

Oh Red Noor,

Allah talks to us through symbols,
And why not realise His Symbolic

'Allah says:
*Sons of
Adam
complain
against
Time, and I
am Time. In
My hand is
the night
and the
day.'*

PROPHET
Muhammad
صلى الله عليه وسلم

All is His
Time and
Space.
Zappy love
is
swimming
in each
planetary
rotation.

La ilaha il Allah

Meaning inside your magnetism

He made you as a Kaba
so that one day a Man may find

and unlock you

An Angel shows him his double. It's him. Kalandar is staring right into himself. He looks at his eyes and sees the image of Noor. He inspects his own hands –they are Noor's hands. His body has become Noor. He, himself, Kalandar standing facing himself-in-her says:

take your shoes off,
let me zonk you out

take my hand in yours
we'll fly to Mars

and I'll talk to you
of the beauty of Venus

and when you're
satisfied and dishevelled

dripping in our
raw glowing embers

our minds full
of spiritual philosophy

I'll bring you into my world,
take you out of your earth

welcome to
your origin

music we'll make out of your black tresses
and drink from our squeezed souls

in this wondrous abode
you become the symbol
of prayer –the Haji's centre,

'Allah says of man: *I am with him when he makes mention of Me. If he makes mention of Me to himself, I make mention of him to Myself.*'

PROPHET
Muhammad
صلى الله عليه وسلم

Extra dimensions are jumping as holographic love is Universally present. Your thoughts activate Reality. Turn your self in towards the One.

muhammad ur rasul allah

the primordial Symbol

*A towering Kaba
that's Scarlet Red
resembling the rose
you threw my way*

*Red by the blood
of your skin scratched
with my claws
heightened by the
ink of a Black Taj Mahal
ablaze in the
wake of my
movement to
your Throne,
oh Mughal Princess*

Kalandar separates from himself-in-her and he becomes
his broken form again.   Her red light diminishes. She sails
to another corner of the universe. In vain Kalandar tries to
call her but to no avail. An angel asks: 'What's the matter?'

Kalandar answers in a
trance:

*Her soul is
my longing*

*empty
space*

*for an
unearthly*

black stone

*yeah,
Hajar al-Aswad,*

space-rock

*She's a Red Kaba
my Soul Mosque*

*In the inner world
of
khayali perception.*

*I yearn a Hajj
to that Red Kaba*

*a love-sick
pilgrim am I!*

'Allah loves
a slave who
is pious,
free of all
wants and
self
concealing.'

PROPHET
Muhammad
صَلَّى اللَّهُ عَلَيْهِ وَسَلَّمَ

Hide your
reality.
Paradoxically
a luminous
forehead
will draw
sincere love
towards
your soul.
Sweet
freedom
arises when
there is no
smoke of
material
possession.
Carefree
living
without
regard to
what
people
think of
you.

'The heaviest thing to be placed in the balance of a believing slave on the Day of Judgement will be good behaviour.'

PROPHET Muhammad صلى الله عليه وسلم

Mould the jelly of your behaviour upon goodness. Polite living is the focal point around which red love's gravity revolves.

The Prophet sal-Allah:
'There are seven
Earths
each with it's own
Kaba.'

When I reach it,
I shall take ghusl,

in Ihram
and flip-flop

I will
enter

the
Gate

to
her
masjid al-Haraam

but
I know

I will
be

turned
away

by the
Angels

of
His Shariah

yet I
will

entreat
Allah

to send

me

His Angels
of

Haqiqah.

they will
lovingly

take me
in their

winged arms
and

wipe my
burning
tears,

They will
shower
attar,

upon my
black
hair,

and kiss
my
full

lips

Allah's beautiful
Angels
of Nurani beauty

with their deepest
brilliant comforting
eyes

will transmute
my body

into a
fresh cloud

of dark
black baraka.

Mika'il the Farishta
of winds will

tenderly carry me
until I hover

above that
Red Red Kaba.

Shariah Angels
look on
at horror

as

Haqiqah Angels
explode me
with love

I become
Black Rain
and blissfully
fall to

the object
of
all
my
wantings.

My scorching
black rain

will bang
desperately

on her

roof

and flow
down

her red
walls.

'It is raining
black!' the pilgrims
cry.

'Sin! Sin!
a sign of sin,'
herald the
Shariah Malaikah

Retorts Mika'il,
Archangel of
Nature:

'Nonsense fools,
black rain
fell to cleanse
her. See how
resplendent each of
her faces has
become. All
of you come to
kiss her stone,
you only see
the outward. But
Black Rain
an ardent lover
who denied by
Shariah, could only
leave his body
and join with
her through soul,
has taught revelation.
All of you
only want Hajj
for your own
deeds but this

'Cheer the
people up
by
conveying
glad tidings
to them.'

PROPHET
Muhammad
صلى الله عليه وسلم

Take steps
to light up
those in
your
vicinity.
Your voice
can contain
the leafy
seed of
hope.

'You are
calling a
Hearer, One
very close
by. The One
Who you
are calling is
closer to
each one of
you.'

PROPHET
Muhammad

Love's
glimmering
star bathes
the
soundless
moonlight.
If you could
see it, you'd
notice the
hands
always
holding
yours.

dark rain is
risking himself to
fill her spirit
with light. Red
Kaba is
gambling with
her soul by
accepting his
water! Oh
Angels, why do
you deny the
two who would
be one sphere?
Can you not
see black on
red, in
time, with Allah's
will, bear fruit?
I understand nature
my angelic dears.'

Jibra'il, the
Archangel of
Revelation opened
his imaginal billion
wings and
stood towering,
his voice
a thunder:
'Mika'il, my
companion Angel.
Usually you
are so
patient! You
know better
than most
if an
alien comes
between Princess
and Prince,
death and
destruction follow.
Come to
your senses

and see
what this
black rain
can do.
Oh Angel
of Nature,
when atoms
love each
other too
much, you
get nuclear
explosion!
All is
destroyed in
its wake!'

Mika'il speaks:
'My dearest
Jibra'il. Don't
you know
the difference
between the
earth and
the spirit?
A body
may love
through spirit
thus bypass
the Earthly
Shariah and
the world.
How could
Allah ever
throw them
into Hell.
Neither did
they force
talaq, nor
did they
leave their
blood bonds.
Oh Jibra'il,
you know
not nature

as I,
Nature's Protector
know it.
Atoms in
love cause
Nuclear Fusion
not Fission.
Atoms give
useful power.
Their energy
will transmute
to baraka,
their vibrations
will light
the world
of Islam.
Red Kaba
without Black
Rain will
be a
tree bearing
no seed.'

This argument
carries on
into the
unsteady morning.

Fajr looms
large on
the horizon...

All pilgrims
Stand in

unspoken awe.
If ever a Hajj
was a spectacle,
this was it.

From the Red
Minarets, a call from
another
dimension. The Feared

One, the Angel of Death.

As his steed comes ever
near, every single one
of
the pilgrims die
one by one. For his
baraka is the baraka
of killing. None is
immune.

The Angel of
Death Himself.

Isra'il, the Archangel's
Lightning face shines:

'You all detest me,
but don't you know
that stars
twinkle because of
the blackness in
night. I kill 'tis true.
Though none of you
see what lies beyond
in the other dimension.
This passionate love
between the Rain and
the Kaba. The man
and the woman. The
active and the passive.
The water and the
earth. The dark
and the light. The
seeker
and the sought.
All loving duality
is from Surah
Yasin: aladhi khalaqal
az waja kulaha mima
tumbitul ardho wa
min an fosihim

'Whoever
remains
patient,
Allah will
make him
patient.
Nobody can
be given a
blessing
better and
greater
than
patience.'

PROPHET
Muhammad

Every drop
of blood
senses your
thoughts. If
given to
patience,
your body
recognises
it as
primordial
and lessens
its impact
towards
illness.
Love's
twinkling
revolution
fills your
body with
Sacred
Healing.
Cool. It's
Baraka.

'I was sent to perfect good character.'

PROPHET
Muhammad

Politeness. Giving way to people. Greeting them. Helping strangers in trouble. The Prophet, upon whom be peace, would always turn fully to people who he would be talking with and would not allow two people to speak a language that the third wouldn't understand. Don't build external statues in public spaces but encourage inner polite behaviour instead.

wa mima la ya'ala-mun,
He has created
pairs in everything
in the earth in
yourselves and in
that which you
do not know.
If Allah himself
has made two
souls from one
entity, it yearns
to unite. Where
is your compassion
Jibra'il?'

Jibra'il opens his
wings, his light
overpowers the black
of Isra'il. All Pilgrims
gain life once more.
His luminous mouth
utters clear words:

'I bring revelation
and that is
my purpose. God
has Himself said
what is good,
what is allowed
and what is
forbidden. What I
speak is not
from my mind:
It's Allah's Shariah
Without Shariah
there is
no Haqiqah.'

Isra'il:
'Allah is Rahman,
and is Raheem,
why do you
not call upon
Allah's Kindness in
your judgements oh
my Brother Arch-Angel?
If I told
you what I
had seen in
the Next Life,
you would reverse
your words oh
white-baraka One!
I have seen
preachers in hell,
and others enter
heaven's fragrant door.'

'*Enough,*' Angelic Isra'fil has entered,
'*I have come to blow*
the Trumpet. Life is
over. Allah will
decide their fate.'

Kalandar wakes up in the middle of the night. He draws what he has seen and writes as much as he can remember on some paper in which some fish and chips were wrapped. Climbs out of the loft window and walks miles and miles to Noor's Office. The cleaners are beginning their early morning predawn shifts. It's not his turn yet but no one notices.

* * *

The next morning, Nana-Abu insists on coming into the office. Noor is surprised by how well versed he is in the world of corporate work.

'Was this all part of your spy training?'

He chuckles: 'I know the British more than the young whippersnappers of today know themselves.'

She enters her office and immediately pushes windows open, 'Smells like someone has been having fish in here.'

She's about to throw the source of the smell located on her chair away. Is startled. Starts reading the poetry and examines the drawings.

She sits at her desk, frozen.

'What is it baytti?'

'This is the dream I had last night. Someone has written it out and even drawn what I saw.'

'Let me see.'

She pulls the papers away, 'Sorry. They will only cause you some distress.'

'You're the one in distress. This is why I came here. You are too much in contact with the spiritual world. You've connected yourself spiritually to another man's soul. Allow me to see the writing. You need peace.'

'I am at peace. What I am reading fills my heart with joy.'

Nana-Abu: 'Joy on earth is shortlived and I have seen it wreck many souls.'

His caring fatherly eyes.

She slowly hands over Kalandar's poems and sketches.

* * *

'Allah says: *I forbid oppression for Myself and have made it forbidden amongst you, so do not oppress one another.*'

PROPHET Muhammad

Captured love is the axis that frees Self. Catch and sniff fragrant petals in love's freedom.

Hu Allah. Vibration of soul upon soul, the alchemy of philosophical and practical happiness

CHAPTER IX

Noor has been loitering around the cleaner's stock cupboard for a while, 'I've been waiting for you Kalandar. It's nice to see you.'

'Seems like years since we last saw each other.'

'Thank you for leaving the wonderful drawings and poems at my desk.'

'I wanted to share the experience with you.'

Noor: 'I think we both had an identical adventure last night. I saw exactly that dream. Isn't it fascinating?'

'It's a real experience. We were in the same world. When I would sit with the Sufi Master Shaykh Junoon, similar things happened.'

'Oh my Allah. You never told me that you had a Sufi Shaykh! Have you told him about us?'

'He's no longer my Mentor. He told me I would find my teacher here in England.'

'Acha?'

'I love it when you go all excited Noor.'

'Psychologists believe that dreams are revealing of personality, but I now understand the truth of the Qur'anic Verse about the soul travelling out of the body when you sleep.'

'The sleep-world is an actual terrain Noor. We go there in our souls.'

'If that is a Reality, which is the more Real? The one we're in or the one we go to?'

'Hmm. Probably both are the same in one sense.'

'If therefore a woman who is married in this world has a romance in the other world with a another man is that punished by Allah?'

'Erm. Shouldn't think so. No. This world is the testing ground. The other worlds are not. At least that's what I feel. But maybe I'm wrong. That's a hard question.'

Noor looks around to see no one is looking then runs her hands through his hair, 'Kalandar, I may only be able to meet you in the virtual space of dreams. Just as last night you transformed into Black Rain, you may have no other option but meet me there.'

'Why?'

'Allah has stated: *Pride is My cloak and greatness My robe, and he who competes with Me in respect to either of them I shall cast into Hell-fire.'*

PROPHET Muhammad

Never feel greater than your Beloved. Pride is His. Not yours. Simply enter the marble chamber and enjoy it. Make it your routine to absorb all the loveliness around you and you'll be so full of oomph, that you won't have space or the desire to become proud.

She rests her head on his chest, 'I don't think there is a future together for us on this earth. Given the current world situation, I feel inclined to support the Muslim Ummah by marrying Prince Freddie.'

Normally Kalandar would have run away, but there is enough of Noor in him that he becomes detached from emotions —for a short while, 'By marrying a man you don't love; how will you influence his mind?'

She looks down to the floor, unable to meet his eyes, 'Freddie has changed already. I spoke to him on the phone today and he's agreed to seriously think of converting to Islam.'

'Just like that?'

'Please don't make it difficult for yourself. It hurts me when you are in pain.'

'If he's converting to marry you isn't that the wrong reason?'

'There are many roads to Allah. As a Sufi you should know that better than me. Please, I'm telling you the truth when I say I don't have feelings for him. It is common for marriages to be arranged —in our families all our marriages were arranged.'

'So you're going the whole route with Prince Fraudey? And have children too?'

Noor: 'Please try to understand me, our memories and companionship can last forever in the spiritual world.'

Kalandar picks up a large black plastic bin, 'I wish I had been born into Royalty and had whiter skin.'

Noor wipes away a reflexive tear, 'Kalandar!'

He shows her the rubbish from the bin, 'I'm just a cleaner. How can you hope to affect the world by marrying me?'

He turns away, striding away from her like a man who has lost *virtually* everything. His only power left on this earth is the ability to feel, 'I thought I would find my rest in your eyes. I should have known you would always remain tomorrow's fantasy, and never today's reality. Who am I to stop you from living the life of luxury and at the same time saving humanity? You seem to be so blessed with everything, and I'm the pebble you've found on the riverbed to throw back after you've played with it a little.'

He doesn't notice her sobbing uncontrollably, so lost is he in his own sense of heightened self-awareness.

* * *

Friday night and Bradford is full of world media.

Ami-ji and the children are decked out in their finest.

The shop is decorated with lights and the carpets have been washed.

An Anti-War demonstration is not allowed anywhere near their street.

Kalandar, Salman and Auntie-ji are watching a broadcast of the proceedings in the living room.

The TV commentary:-

Studio: *So... when are we expected to see Prince Freddie and where are you reporting from?*

Reporter: *I'm actually outside the street where Miss Noor grew up. The whole area as you can see behind me has been cordoned off. No one is allowed anywhere near her Parental home. Bradford City Centre is teeming with Police. We have had reports of arrests but nothing serious. As far as seeing His Royal Highness the Prince of Wales, well our cameras do have access to his motorcade and we'll be able to see him step out onto the red carpet.*

Studio: *Am I right in saying that an announcement is about to be made.*

Reporter: *Yes, that's right Jonathon. We are expecting an important statement from Prince Freddie himself.*

Studio: *There is speculation that marriage could be in the air?*

Reporter: *Yes that's right. We are all on tenterhooks. It has also been leaked out that the Prince has converted to Islam. Now this is pure speculation.*

Studio: *What are Palace sources saying?*

Reporter: *Obviously the Palace is cautious and if it is true, and the Prince has converted to Islam, then a lot of constitutional issues arise. I've tried to talk to sources close to the Windsor Family and everyone is tight-lipped –but the fact that they have not denied it is leading to a lot of questions.*

Studio: *Like for instance: Would it be possible to have a Muslim King when the state religion is Church of England?*

Reporter: *Yes, that's absolutely right. And also there could be calls for a republic too. Will the monarchy survive in today's England? Prince Freddie is an extremely popular prince and we know he wants to be King. He will not abdicate his throne, nor will the Queen accept anyone but Freddie. But let's not jump to conclusions.*

'Allah has said: *O My servants, you sin by night and by day, and I forgive all sins, so seek forgiveness of Me and I shall forgive you.*'

PROPHET Muhammad

Forgiveness is the vehicle to cross love's leggy landscape. Stay in there if you want to reach the Kaba.

Studio: *Indeed. We'll just cross over to our cameras. Live. I can see Prince Freddie getting out of the car, with him is his bodyguard. Jonathon, why do you think he has chosen to talk to the media here.*

Reporter: *Well. Like I said before he's a well-liked Royal and this is partly because of his closeness to the people. By coming here into one of the most multi-ethnic areas of England and also one of the poorest, he's sending a clear signal that he is, as he has always said he is – the People's Prince.*

Studio: *Can I stop you for a moment. We can see young Miss Noor. She's wearing a traditional blue dress and has taken her place with the Prince. We can hear what he has to say. Live from Bradford.*

The Prince coughs and splutters a little, jokingly looks to his left at Noor and announces his intent clearly: 'Respected audience. Citizens of the Commonwealth and my friends and family. I would like to greet you with a few wonderful words that young Noor here has taught me. *As-salam alaikum.* This means *Peace be upon you.* I beg to wish peace upon you and upon the hospitable family of Noor. I am here today to announce not only my conversion to the Islamic faith but also my engagement to the most beautiful woman I have ever met. She is as delightful on the inside as she is pretty in the face. Together we hope to create, not only a new life, but also a new peaceful world. Thank you everyone.'

Freddie leaves.

Hordes of Reporters throughout the world begin calling, e-mailing and screaming into their phones. Noor is now the focal point of the entire world.

* * *

Kalandar is sitting at the kitchen table wondering how his father is doing. With the war, it's difficult to get accurate information. If only his mother hadn't died. Maybe he would have turned out different. There's only his father left to think about since Noor is marrying Freddie after all. Soon he will have to leave Uncle-ji Salman's house and his job as a cleaner too. But where would he go?

Farah and Nadeem both enter together. To mock him, Farah plays a Bollywood wedding song, 'Saajanji ghar aya hae.'

'Let him who finds good, praise Allah and let him who finds other than that, blame no one but himself.'

PROPHET Muhammad

It is your reaction to life that gives it quality. Look with the gaze of brushed love so that you may blame none.

Nadeem catches his attention with a sneer, 'As salaam alaikum Sir. How are you today Saab-ji?'

Kalandar says nothing. Stands up. Angry. Walks out of the house.

Auntie-ji, 'Nadeem, what's wrong with Kalandar?'

'Probably needs some air, it can't be much fun sniffing toilet shit all day.'

'Don't be so mean! What if he gets lost again?'

'He won't. He's such a greedy pukha. He always seems to know where to eat roti.'

They don't realise that he has overheard them. He was delayed fumbling with opening the front door.

He runs and runs. Runs as far as his lungs can cope. Sits, burnt out outside a graveyard. His attuned sense can make out the ghosts of people floating around. How he wishes he was as free as them.

Then he remembers Noor's words. She talked about meeting in the spirit world. His hatred towards Freddie overwhelms him. He wishes he could take Noor's memory out of his heart, but when he tries, he only remembers her more.

'I'll eat nothing. Eat nothing until I become a skeleton like Majnun,' he says to himself.

* * *

Early Morning newspaper headlines:

Frantic Freddie Furore.

No Islam please we're British

Daft Freddie: Call me Fareed.

Foolish Fred. Go ahead.
Wear your Moslem Burka – we WON'T.

Naughty Nasty Noor:
gorgeous glamour girl
or suicide bomber?

Freddie watch out:
You're too gay to be Moslem

'Allah has stated, *My servant continues to draw near to Me with extra works so that I love him. When I love him I am his hearing with which he hears, his seeing with which he sees, his hand with which he strikes and his foot with which he walks.'*

PROPHET
Muhammad

Fresh love is the juice that fills your body with Divine Secrets.

> 'Allah declares: *If My servant likes to meet Me, I like to meet him; and if he dislikes to meet Me, I dislike to meet him.'*
>
> **PROPHET** Muhammad
>
>
>
> Yearn Allah. The sign of love is when your beloved's name enters your heart, something inside you moves. It melts the metal of your whole being. Don't love for what Allah will give, rather love Him as His Essence is Alluring. If you haven't realised it yet, then who put love in your heart in the first instance?

**Treason. Hang Mad Prince
Who has betrayed Britain
to the Taliban**

* * *

It's Monday and it's 4pm. Still no sign of Kalandar.

Noor is really worried. He's not returned any of her calls, nor turned up for work.

His Supervisor tells her that Kalandar's Uncle phoned in to say he's missing from home.

Noor feels a strange presence. Forgets her own self and runs to the lift. She knows he is somewhere nearby. Her heart can sense him. He's so close... In her office, she feels him. Sprints quickly and sees a silver object wrapped in a brown paper bag. It's the phone she bought him! He's returned it with what seems like his own blood smeared over it. Looks out of the window.

She prays the verse of the Qur'an for finding lost items, 'Ina lillahi wa inna alayhi raji-un.'

It's Kalandar!

He's running. Bustling against traffic on the wrong side of the road.

She falls down the stairs, injuring her feet.

To the astonishment of the entrance receptionists and security staff, she runs barefoot out into the crowded capital. He scampers down the tube station and leaps over the barrier (he needs to be careful he doesn't get shot dead by police). Onto a tube train.

She can't see him but knows he's hurtling away at speed. She jumps on the next carriage. Praying 'Ya Wujuudo!' *Oh Sought Being.*

He gets off at the next stop and finds a fountain. *Great!* He dives in headfirst. The impact splatters muddy splashes over annoyed tourists.

She thinks, 'Water...water...' and spots a sign to the Thames. Her long skirt gets wet as she walks, gasping for breath, 'No he's not here.'

Out of the fountain, a soaked, barely breathing Kalandar climbs a tree. Exasperated, he falls asleep in thick branches near a bird's nest.

Tired and grubby, Noor has a vision of birds and trees. She looks and sees countless trees lining the busy road.

She wheezes and whines heavily.

Catches a glimpse in a shop window at her torn clothes. *At least no one will recognise me. Life is getting hard enough being on the cover of each newspaper.* Walks into a shop, changes her clothes and decides to take the day off.

Her heart is pounding, Ya Allah, *Ya Salaam*, Give me Peace.

* * *

'Allah affirms: *I have prepared for My righteous servants what no eye has seen and no ear has heard, nor has it occurred to the human heart.*'

PROPHET Muhammad

Beauty behind the veil of this universe is past compare. What you see are glitzy love signals of the Real.

You are what you feel you are. Contemporary drama is flushed with
yesterday's paint. Time is a temporary creature.

CHAPTER X

Days pass and Kalandar lives off brackish water in a verdant grassy part of a public park making implements of wood. Banging his frustration out on stones and rocks.

Currently Noor is seriously ill. And a concerned Prince Freddie has her admitted into a clinic on Harley Street.

Today is the day of the largest demonstration of British Pakistani men and women since the Rushdie affair.

The march of anti-war protestors is presently at a standstill outside the Palace. There's a man with a handmade bow and arrow in the moving throng.

It's Kalandar.

He's starving and emaciated, but intent on killing Prince Freddie. *Why should we make love to the goray?* Look at them, they have our lands and now openly make love to our women.

He moves like a cheetah, hidden amidst the rising clang of shouts and slogans. And has heard there is a party on in the Palace. That Freddie is there.

Noor turns over in the hospital bed. She hasn't eaten for days either. Horrified at the thoughts she's feeling from Kalandar. 'Must prevent death. Must save the Prince. Where is Fareed?'

She hurriedly phones the Prince. *Shit! Buckingham Palace. Why on earth is he staying there today?* Closes her eyes. *Yes – that's it. That's where Kalandar is also. Oh no, he has a weapon!*

Tells the security guard it's a matter of life and death. Soon she is wheeling towards the Palace. The roads are blocked. Not even the Royal Pass can take her past Police Lines.

Jumps out of the car, encircled by security guards. They plead for Noor to stop.

'Don't even think of touching me!' she screams and ignores their shouts.

At the hidden entrance to the Palace.

'Let me in! Let me in!'

Soon she's with the Prince. 'Please do not go outside. Please don't go outside.'

'By assisting your wives in their household matters you men receive the reward of charity.'

PROPHET
Muhammad
صَلَّى اللّٰهُ عَلَيْهِ وَسَلَّم

Bizarre modern society puts work at the centre of life. Asymmetric and ugly. Undo this broken symmetry by reflecting in each other. Beauty and balance can be yours if you create harmony of *Rahmaniya* feminine and *Malikiya* masculine.

He's jovial and finds her funny.

Freddie-Fareed steps out of the balcony to hear the protestors. An arrow whizzes from nowhere. She dives to protect him. The wooden stump ends up in Noor's body. In agony, she slumps to the ground. A hint of a smile on her face as she sees Freddie-Fareed is alive.

* * *

They quickly locate Kalandar weeping and wailing openly, 'I've killed her. I've killed her.'

Police take him.

He's put into maximum security.

* * *

'Will she survive?' Prince Freddie-Fareed's face is grey.

The Doctor shakes her head. 'The injury is deep. She's lost blood. I'm sorry.'

He looks at her beautiful face.

'She was nice. She was so bloody nice,' the Prince bangs his fist on the table. Swears many an extraordinary expletive.

* * *

Dark solid cold cell.

Kalandar's head between his knees.

Oh Allah. How could I have shot my Noor. Oh Allah. My hands have wounded my Noor. Allah! Allah! Mujhe Maaf karo. Noor. Hai Noor. Kia kar diya meh nae?

* * *

Nana-Abu may soon seem to have changed to you dear reader. But don't you know, he, like other elders, were once young and flirted (with death too) on many an occasion. Don't ever think that so called 'immigrants' in poor houses haven't seen glory or have had their share of the world. He was at the partition. In like manner, he became embroiled in

'The best of wealth is a righteous woman who pleases her husband when he sees her.'

PROPHET
Muhammad
صَلَّى اللهُ عَلَيْهِ وَسَلَّم

A pleasing face and a beautiful countenance is abundant wealth. So blessed be the wealthy who have found unfailing erotic human love, however fractal it may seem to theologians.

the hidden war between the relatives of the Old Osmanlari against the young Turks. He was causing further intrigue in Bosnia and Kabul. But could not help any fellow Aristocrat.

He's at the bedside of Noor. With a heavy voice: 'Prince Fareed, there is one way we can cure dear Noor.'

'Which is?'

'Someone has to die in her place.'

Tearful Freddie-Fareed: 'Is this a Muslim thing?'

'It's the Mughal way. When the son of Babar, the one who was to become Emperor Humayun was on his deathbed, all healers had pronounced him incurable. Babar implored Allah to take his life and save his son.'

'Likewise, I lay down my soul for my Beloved Noor.'

'No my dear Prince. Call that dastardly would-be assassin. The ugly, irascible Kalandar. Call him here and we will see what sort of man he is. Is he prepared to die a hero?'

'How can I? He's now in Police custody.'

'You're a Prince aren't you? When will someone in this country, where horses and donkeys are considered equal, listen to a man of Noble lineage? You were born to rule by God.'

'It would break the constitution.'

'Look. Even the Archbishop of Canterbury is privately supporting your succession despite you being a Muslim. There is something in your blood that makes it a necessity that you command the British Isles. Be firm now and break the will of the Parliamentarians and their hoodlum partners at Whitehall. Bring back the Kingdom. Return to your rightful status as Absolute Monarch.'

'Easier said than done my old friend.'

'Your mother is Head of State. If you love Noor you will have Kalandar brought here in chains. Oh Prince.'

* * *

Kalandar's breathing is shallow. But he can see that he is no longer in his cell.

'Where am I?'

Nana-Abu: 'So you're the pathetic Panjaabi faqeer. All that is left of the Lohdi clan. A love-struck madman. Whimpering like a dog at my heel. I have no idea how you won my grand daughter's heart but if you value your

'Your adorning and beautifying yourselves for your husbands and your strivings to please your husbands and your doing the wishes of your husbands equals theirs in rewards.'

PROPHET Muhammad صلى الله عليه وسلم

Thus spoke the Holy Apostle to Asma who was worried that men seem to have more opportunities than women to do religious service. Even that which is done within the geography of passionate love has merit in front of Allah.

chivalry; you will die for her. Are you a Javaan Mard or coward?'

'Please go easy old fruit. This is England not India...'

Nana-Abu pretends to overlook the Prince's remark.

He brings his mouth to Kalandar's ear: 'Aaap nae marna hae? Toh pihrrr Noor kay liyay maro. Panah mahngoh Khuda sae. Beseech Allah that He may sacrifice you in Noor's place.'

Kalandar gets up and asks for water. He can't keep his bloodshot eyes off Noor's inert body. Life-support machinery hums monotonously into his ears.

Nana-Abu pulls a cloth over Noor's hair, 'You have no right to see her. She is not yours.' Then with unexpected gentleness helps Kalandar to his feet and lays a musalla for him. Nana-Abu is no cruel tyrant; he kisses Kalandar between his eyes and then turns away for the inevitable.

Kalandar uses all the powers of spiritual concentration made available, calls out to Allah. Forces his earthly life out of his soul and his body energy to be deposited into Noor's heart.

She opens her eyes as he closes his.

* * *

'Made beloved to me from your world are women and perfume, and the coolness of my eyes is in prayer.'

PROPHET Muhammad ﷺ

Virtual symmetries of this world have been made to be loved. Sensual strokes on this globe can connect with Transcendent Otherness. The paradox continues.

All, but the Face of your Noble Majestic Lord, is perishable nothingness.

a Sufi Love Story

CHAPTER XI

The doctors rush in and consider the full recovery a remarkable miracle.

Noor herself is in bed and confined to the hospital room.

Freddie-Fareed takes her hand and sobs gently.

She suddenly feels a sense of closeness to him. *He cares. He actually cares.*

Nana-Abu is in Sajda, facing the Sacred City of Makka.

Noor: 'What happened?'

The Prince removes his hand. 'The unthinkable my lady. Thank God, or should I say Thank Allah?'

'Both describe the same Being.'

'Your Grandfather saved the day.'

All has forgotten the lifeless limp body of Kalandar.

All that is, except for Noor.

'It's Kalandar!'

'He can't harm you no more. He is dead.'

'Who killed him?'

Freddie-Fareed hesitates and then closes his mouth.

Nana-Abu sits up and plainly states the facts:

'He prayed that Allah put his soul at His Mercy so that you might live. It was an act of selflessness I'll give him that. But as a condemned man in both worlds it was his only option.'

'No-o-o!' Noor gets up and drops by his head.

She puts her hand and sends baraka to his heart.

Nana-Abu pulls her away, 'Do not die for him. The deed has been done.'

Prince Freddie calls for Kalandar's body to be removed.

* * *

Clouds gather overhead.

It seems as if the sun may hide behind them forever.

* * *

Aziz Mustapha Khan & Sons often have to dispose of Muslim bodies that for whatever reason haven't been claimed by relatives and loved ones.
Kalandar's body is being readied at the mortuary.
The funeral parlour manager, Aziz, can sense the beginnings of a breath.
He catches Kalandar's eyes flickering.
But he knows that this is the man who tried to kill the Prince.
Aziz, himself a descendant of a Pathan fighter doesn't trust the authorities. In his eyes, Kalandar is a hero. He takes off his coat, wraps it around Kalandar and takes him to his own family.

* * *

Six weeks is a long time to have an unknown man in your house.
Especially when that man has lost all memories.
Aziz watches Kalandar playing with the family cat. Perhaps losing his memory is a blessing in disguise, he thinks and then decides that he should get Kalandar something to do.

* * *

Clarence House has gardens attended to personally by Prince Freddie-Fareed. Noor daily walks the length and breadth of the rose garden especially planted in her honour. But neither the haunting beauty of the garden, nor the presence of Nana-Abu can detract her from the loss of Kalandar.
Noor is wearing white.
She no longer wears red. Has visited what she has been told is his grave but never once felt his spiritual presence there. She remembers how in happier times Kalandar would wince uneasily and then manage to grin that raw innocent smile when she would tease him. *The conversations in her office.* The day she gave him a rose

'Verily there are heavenly rewards for any act of kindness to a living creature.'

PROPHET Muhammad ﷺ

Go stroke a cat. Feed a hungry bird. Rays of clear love connect you with every entity on this planet. Smile.

Raise your eyes and make them grin and cackle, humouring your spiritual associates. Cheerful gentle expressions empower the space between humans and blesses the aura between them.

and he had no idea what to do with it. Moments all drowned in memories. They didn't spend much time together. Regret is a new emotion for her.

She is swinging gently on a canopy-swing, her white silk flowing with her.

Nana-Abu: 'You have become a Mughal Princess, as was your nature.'

'Ji, how could you have done what you did? I can't believe you ordered Kalandar to die.'

'It's been months yet you can't move on! Maeri baytti. This world is a cruel place. Have you not heard the story of Khizr, who slew a youth for the sake of his parents?'

'How could you? I've always grown to respect you as my teddy bear. As the gentlest man in the world.'

'Noor Rani... The saving of the life of a Princess is preferable to the saving of a Peasant.'

'It was this attitude that allowed the British into India in the first place Nana-ji. The Maharajas trod on the poor. Doesn't the Qur'an state the killing of one life is like the killing of entire humanity? Remember Bilal? The great scholar who Prophet Muhammad, *sal-Allaho*, elevated from the rank of a mere slave to the greatest Muazdhin in Islam?'

'We are not the Maharaja. Nor do we believe in Hindu caste systems. We are Mughals, the rightful Protectors of the Indian peoples. Darling Noor! Please listen to me. The British History books and the modernist Islamic textbooks you read are written by inexperienced illiterate buffoons. They can't be relied on.'

She stares into empty space, 'And– doesn't the Qur'an Majeed talk against human sacrifice? That the blood of sacrifice does not reach Allah but your intention?'

'My Noor, my intention was good, both for you and for Kalandar. Soon you will realise. Soon.'

* * *

Kalandar should really be described as a man with no memory. It would be wrong to label him a walking zombie.

Aziz: 'I think it's time you did something with your life. Perhaps a job or a college course?

'Of all lawful acts the most detestable to Allah is divorce.'

PROPHET Muhammad صَلَّى اللَّهُ عَلَيْهِ وَسَلَّمَ

Oneness in everything is the way of the resilient snow-flower. Separation between two who have once joined is blue ruin. Spells and magic to divide woman and man abound. Protect yourselves through Allah.

'I want to go to Pakistan and fight the Allied forces. In my heart there is a residual memory of the Panjaab: dust roads, parched soil, milk of Water Buffalo, echo of the Azaan. I can sense the magnificence of Lahore in my bones. I may not remember the details but the taste of the Panjaab lingers in the depths of my mind.'

'I admire you. And I can get you there.'

* * *

Six months pass and Kalandar proves himself to be a worthy fighter. His beard is thick and long. The Turban at his head is smeared with the grime of the many tanks he has captured. Shrapnel in his thighs makes it difficult for him to walk. His right shoulder seems as if Wildebeest have stomped on it. You see, the way an exploding AK47 smashes into your bones doesn't just leave bruises.

* * *

Noor is in New York.

In a private chamber the PM of Britain is tearing his hair out (and he didn't have much to begin with either).

'Princess we cannot accept your resolution.'

She runs a slender hand down her full-length glossy hair, 'Resolution 28.9-Aii declares the war on Pakistan as an unsanctioned invasion. The continued occupation is illegal as is the holding of Prisoners. It violates almost every single UN charter on human rights.'

'You sound more like a hardnosed lawyer than a Princess.'

'I am a lawyer.'

'Plus, you are royalty and do you know – you're putting your husband's position in jeopardy? You are perilously close yourself in violating what the royals can and cannot get involved in.'

'I represent not only the royal family but also the people of Great Britain. They don't want war. The Prince and I do have support.'

'God is pure and loves purity and cleanliness.'

PROPHET Muhammad ﷺ

Purify your clothes, your body, your mind and the place you live in. Clean every part you can. Purity and love is an indivisible twisted rope that holds two lovers upon the swing of Permanence.

'Verily God has more compassion for His creatures, than this mother for her own child.'

PROPHET Muhammad ﷺ

The Prophet spoke the above after asking the Noble Companions if a woman would ever throw her own child into fire. Too much talk of hell darkens the soul. And it detracts from the unbounded love of Allah.

'Be that as it may, even if I wanted to bring our troops home we can't. In fact I'm flying out to Pakistan in a few hours time to assess the situation,' stares at her body through his dark glasses, 'if the Princess would care to join me?'

'And convince you to pull our boys out.'

'Nay, you'll see at first hand what'd happen if we left. There would be worse bloodshed than the partition. We must hold out for as long as it takes for terrorist bases to be destroyed and the Taliban annulled. I won't give up so easily.'

Noor puts down her briefing notes, 'And neither will I Prime Minister. I accept your offer. When do you fly out to Pakistan?'

* * *

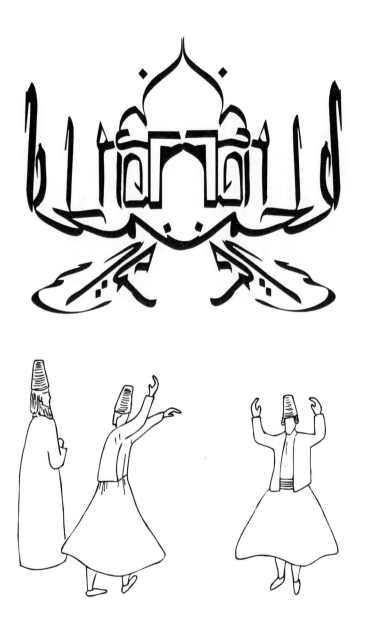

Spin out of **this**, welcoming the future of **that**.

CHAPTER XII

'When any
action
pricks your
conscience,
leave it.'

PROPHET
Muhammad
صلى الله عليه وسلم

Your heart
is an
interface to
Reality.
Cleansed
souls are
full of love's
infinity
– and
instantly
recognise
pain of
delusional
unreality.

Badshahi Masjid, Lahore.

In its shadow, a UN Envoy has been captured.

The guerrilla leader responsible can only speak Urdu. They don't realise that they have caught both the Prime Minister of England (he looks even uglier without make up) and the Princess (she looks more beautiful than on the cameras).

And there is only one captive who can understand him.

Noor: 'Ham Pakistan ko Azaad karnay hi aaa-ay thae..'

He grunts and takes her to one side. She is too pleasant and beautiful to be left with the other hostages.

'Aap meray saath chalo, mae aap ko kutch khaana daeta huu.'

She eats a bit of the offered naan bread. As she does, she hears a motorbike coming to a standstill. Sees a hairy untidy bearded man sharing dates and almonds with young children.

A gulp at her throat.

Noor freezes.

Her head is swimming.

Hazy clouds of nebulous thoughts emerge. Too many. She feels like a child. Her eyes contract then dilate.

It's Kalandar.

She can smell his atmosphere.

Her Captor grabs her arm. But Kalandar has seen her too.

His own memories come flooding back. He staggers back. Falls.

A burst of Love-Adrenaline kick starts his system. He gets up and demands her release.

Men begin murmuring.

It seems as if this human hissing fizzle is enough for the kidnapper to reluctantly let her go.

It all seems so surreal. She finds herself clinging onto Kalandar as the motorbike roars on the dusty roads of Pakistan. He shouts out what happened, over the din of the old bike's spluttering engine. His jealousy at Freddie-

Fareed. His bow and arrow. His jail cell. But most of all, he remembers in vivid detail the moment her hand called his spirit back. He describes the graciousness of The Angel of Death from a distance. The Angel waved him back to earth.

'I saw him too,' she says, but knows he can't hear her – he's so carried away. Puts her head close to his back and holds onto his torso. Kalandar speeds along the dirt track. He can hear the bombs falling around them, not bothering to take cover. Noor doesn't care either.

* * *

'I really don't know what came over me, or what I am doing with a weapon in my hand,' Kalandar's head is leaning by the side of a tree.

A fire is burning in the open.

'This is where the ones who are fighting for Pakistani independence sleep and share stories. You can see men with broken limbs and daughters who have no parents. Their honour is protected as is the defence of our nation. I'm not a terrorist, I don't lay bombs nor kill people but defend the poor. Have you seen what the foreign soldiers do? They have some sick habits.'

'I know you are no killer. You haven't changed. Don't worry about what you did in London. You reacted in the only way you could. I've forgotten it honestly.'

The burning question on Kalandar's mind, 'Are you now married?'

'No.'

'Why not?'

'I've been in mourning.'

'For whom?'

'For you.'

He looks stupidly towards her.

Then, she giggles.

* * *

With the morning sun comes the arrival of American and British soldiers. The rebels put up solid resistance.

'We are about to lay down our lives,' Kalandar has come back to warn her.

'The best of charity is that which springs from the heart, and is uttered by the lips to soften the wounds of the injured.'

PROPHET Muhammad ﷺ

Love's effects are on the tip of your tongue. Humanity is waiting for such a person. Spread soaring words of smoothness so that smiles are left in your wake.

'There is no
monasticism
in Islam.'

PROPHET
Muhammad

Do not turn
away from
love
sensations.
Enjoy all
Names of
Allah as you
feel their
effects.
There is
truth
behind the
world and
in all of its
dazzling
colour and
dynamism.
Touch,
taste and
involve your
soul with
people and
palaces
without
being
affected by
their pulling
power.

Noor: 'I can't believe I lost you once. Why can't you cease fire and hold a truce?'

'It is unIslamic to surrender.'

'Suicide is not part of Islam!'

'This isn't suicide.'

'It's not martyrdom. Kalandar! If there was some purpose only then it would be noble. Don't die needlessly and don't kill any human beings – they are only young British and Americans; they need guidance.'

'Young men who are paid a lot of money. Soldiers? Pfah! I would call them mercenaries.'

She thinks fast, 'I'm trying to bring an end to the conflict. Do you want any more orphaned girls here in Lahore?'

'No!'

She grabs his shoulders.

'Then use me as a hostage. Get some benefit from me. Exchange me for some of the wrongly imprisoned Musalmaan. I'm a Princess and have a lot of value. This way I can continue to pursue diplomatic means to stop the bloodshed. Either I can die with you right now or fathers get to leave jail and care for their families.'

Kalandar is lost in thought.

Noor reads his mind, 'I love you.'

Kalandar has seen too many deaths. He does what Noor has advised.

Soon, they are sitting alone together in the back of a UN jeep.

'What is to become of our lives?' Kalandar asks her.

'There will always be the world standing as a brick wall between us. This dunya is not ours.'

'You once said that we would be forced to meet in the spiritual realm.'

'Yes. It is our destiny. And surely the ruhani realm is a more pleasant place than this zameen.'

'I see what you say.'

'And I feel your pain,' Noor strokes his hand.

'Will we ever meet again?'

'We are so far apart. I can't remain in Pakistan. And you can't come to England – you will be tried for murder. Also, I hate to say this, but after I'm married, according to Shariah, we will never be able to meet up like this.'

Kalandar: 'Allaho ma-asabireen, it's from the Qur'an. Allah is with the patient.'

'You can now recite ayats!'

'I received knowledge from you.'

'And in the process I learnt to use insight. You changed me Kalandar.'

The beginnings of a *final goodbye* begin to emanate from her eyes.

'Inshallah you will change England?'

'My humble faqeer! The West has conquered outer space and reached the moon but through what you've taught me they'll learn to inhabit inner space. They may be able to travel hundreds of miles in their cars, but they seldom visit their own neighbours and mothers. Your soul has entered mine and shown me there is love in raw human spirit. You haven't just talked empty words, but shown me Allah. Your healing will cleanse the modern world.'

'I told you I was the best healer this side of the galaxy.'

'You did indeed.' A smile plays upon the lips but she cannot hide the sadness in her voice.

He can see her waiting plane taxiing on the tarmac.

Kalandar: 'If we separate we will cease to learn from each other.'

'We won't part company. We'll still be together.'

'How can we meet up in the spirit world when we're both without a Shaykh? We need guidance and training.'

She takes out a tatty book from her inner jacket pocket, 'Now that you can read, have this. I found it in the private royal library at Clarence House.'

'What is it?'

'An old Sufi textbook on joining two separated Lovers together. In the spiritual world. I'd been trying to use the methods to contact you. Let Allah Himself be our Shaykh. Perhaps if we both persist with a positive outlook we may be able to meet and feel the Divine Presence too.'

She needs to go to the plane, 'We will meet together inshallah. Every night in the dream world and every morning in Muraqbah.'

He finally understands. And kisses the Bismillah on the cover of the book.[23]

'No more fighting,' he mutters to himself. 'I will walk barefoot to Makka and discover my soul.'

'That person is not of me who makes another a eunuch, or becomes one himself.'

PROPHET
Muhammad

The way of total green love is the path of Fitrah. Destroy not the inborn instinct, utilise it for good.

He is Al-Wadud, the Loving. Love alters letters and is the motor of life.

'The asceticism of my followers is to live in the world and yet to sit in the corner of a mosque also.'

PROPHET
Muhammad

Engage yourself with this unreal world plus set your sight on the After-World. This phenomenal dunya is a symbolic book requiring your brain to dislodge itself from fascination with its patterns. Turn to the Pattern-Designer. Perchance you may gain deeper insight.

A Year Later...

Noor is instrumental in ending the West's war against the Muslim Ummah. She wins an amnesty for all political prisoners. The Palace is fast becoming a place of Prayer. Mughal influence is in every direction, from the new domes erected at Windsor to the Prince Fareed Mosque in London –an exact copy of the *Badshahi*. She may in time become the Mughal Princess who would save the West from materialism.

Kalandar is in a cave but resides in the soul's thought-palace. His senses are under his control. There is no hint of other-than-He. His seven souls and his physical body are at his service. He is a Prince of himself. A perfect man.

* * *

Her purified heart resonates with His Attribute *Kareem*, Generous. Meanwhile the man receives a ray of His Wisdom, *Hakeem*. United they taste the shadow of Infinity.

106

Chapter XIII

It is *Lailatul Qadr*. The Night of Power. Somewhere in
the Himalayan mountains, Kalandar is facing Makka. Body
absorbed in Muraqbah.

In a polished marble hall, Noor is motionless in her bed.
Her figure a perfect statue amongst the silken drapes. Soft
sounds of 'Allahu Allahu' warm the chamber.

She falls as her soul travels out. Her spirit body looks
down and sees her physical body still in the palace bed. She
can see countless Angels zooming in the atmosphere.
Dazzling light is falling far and wide. She feels a coagulation
of baraka-energy. Knows that it is the sign of an open portal
to another world.

'Kill not
your hearts
with excess
of eating
and
drinking.'

PROPHET
Muhammad

Delight
every short
meeting in
presence of
the loved
one. Be not
impatient
for more,
nor delve
into the
world for a
fix to your
pleasure
centres.

A gate opens by an alien looking wingless Farishta.

Waterlike substance is in the ether. She finds herself dressed in Red Mughal robes and angels carry the trailing hem behind her.

In the distance a familiar shape.

It is the mystical luminosity of the Black Taj Mahal.

Her spirit-skin is glowing red and her eyes brown. Black long tresses twirl around her entire body. She finds herself looking down at her reflection. It's as if her hair has surrounded the entire sky and has shunted the three dimensions of distance.

There is a white speck in the centre of the Black Mausoleum.

It's Kalandar.

She hears Angels talking in verse:

the magnetism
of beautiful
alluring Kaba
pulls in
his black
baraka cloud

fateful Juma
gems sparkle
eager anticipation
on her
ear rings

juicy tenseness
in anticipation of
an imploding
full mountain

in its
cave two
icicles lie
untouched

dripping years
forgotten moons

'Do you love your Creator? Love your fellow creatures first.'

PROPHET
Muhammad

Lasting Love bursts forth from the fresh air of your Being. Irresistibly feeding each particle in your proximity.

unaware of
His Oneness

Allah pioneered
two creatures
from one
undifferentiated soul

two confused,
perplexed circles
inexorably clashing

When you catch
the orb of a glance,
your insides begin
to rush into the field

'It is He who created you
from one soul and made
from it its spouse
that he might find
rest in her,'
Qur'an 7:189

'He created you of
a single soul,
then from it He
appointed its spouse,'
Qur'an, 39:6

man woman
woman man

interchangeable
yet so different

sharing Name 'Allah'

98 Attributes left:

49 female signs
49 signs male

yin yang

'Shall I not
inform you
of a better
act than
fasting,
charity, and
prayer?
Making
peace
between
one
another:
enmity and
malice tear
up heavenly
rewards by
the roots.'

PROPHET
Muhammad

All know
that
religious
work brings
Him closer,
yet who
truly
believes
that
spreading
cloudless
love and
silver
serenity
between
humanity
has a
greater
effect?

fusion

Ya-sin
of Qur'an:

'we have created your self in pairs'

raining soil Adam
moving air Eve

globe spinning
Kaba anchoring

She alights and walks to the glimmering silver haired man reclining on a couch, being poured fragrant glowing water by Angels.

His skin is jet black, but his eyes are as she remembers them. His brown iris welcomes the snow of her pleasure.

She spots an empty couch and watches his eyes follow the graceful trail of her hair and he gazes at her whole. Her winged shoes transform into glowing hennaed patterns upon her feet.

With his night-black tongue, he touches the luminous water of the diamond goblet and his flavour is then passed between Noor's lips.

In that moment the water quenches her through poetry; every word-vibration is felt by her entity:

we're
electric
current

in unification
we glow

fruity daylight
seeding baraka

no escaping
angelic flutter

time eternally
pouring lights
into space

between us

in separation, there are streams
of whirlwinds causing havoc

only silenced when
our atoms bang into

one point

Her sip has turned the water red; the Angel swoops to offer it to Kalandar. Her poetry fills his mouth and then shoots into his insides:

My grief
is unspoken

Protect my red hailstones
in your musky black light

We two beings
in apart worlds

loud masculinity
shouts volumes
when your eyes
touch me

the world's only
beheld white light
never your sheer illuminated
deep darkness.

So when a bit of dark light
chanced to shed upon me,

my essence jumped
out-self the floating form

becoming the
swimming
dot in your
letter 'nuun'

'The Lord does not consider prayer in which the heart doesn't accompany body.'

PROPHET
Muhammad

Think not that the beloved's body or surface personality is the most important – think of what lies beyond the attraction you have. After climbing the mountain of the body, ascend the sky of space.

a Sufi Love Story

La ilaha il Allah

'Have
aspiration
that is
high.'

PROPHET
Muhammad

Aspire to
the loftiest
most
magical
love
imaginable.

Behind the screen
of our names,

refreshingly
cold and hot

pristine panorama

frozen wet rain rays
kissingly beaming down

made clear due to
your black brightness

flavoured by the sweet
nectar of universal deer

an incredible musk
whose heady fragrance

races upon
silver desire

you
are

pure
metal
lovingly
wrapped
around
the
hand
of
my
body

each of your thought-rings
upon my fingers
testifies to the wonder

of Divine Oneness.
Allah. Allah. Allah.

'I am the One I love,
and the One I love is I'

Red transmutes black,
Black into Red

enraptured as I am,
by your dimension

I cease living
in my body

the cosmos
alters into
your face

Allah blew into the human being
His 'own spirit' (Qur'an 15:29)
as Allah desires
to be known...
Himself
... His own spirit.

Wave Breaths
Of the
All-Merciful

rehmat
conferred.

When you
breathe into
my spirit

I return
To primordial
Breath implanted

...love into Adam

animalistic nafs:
I want your body

Ruhani nafs:

'Shall I tell
you the
very worst
among you?
Those who
eat alone,
and whip
the slaves,
and give to
nobody.'

PROPHET
Muhammad

Clouds of
misty
enchanting
love remain
yours. Be
connected
to
humanity.
Neglect
nobody.

I want your soul

one wants the
body's pleasure,
the other the
heart's home,

my dear Black,
be my Palace.

'He who
knows his
self, knows
God.'

PROPHET
Muhammad
صلى الله عليه وسلم

He has turned the water black again and so Noor gratefully receives it, her eyes filling up with blackness as she does:

May your red blood
Sweep my black monsoon

Your Self
has a billion
starry
connections
enabling
you to surf
the entire
Universe
and
beyond.
Why don't
you
transform
and morph
into Love's
Centre?

worlds of
Rehmat stem
from our
love of
the beloved
Muhammad

coagulate

allow me
To unveil
Your self
Destroying
My own

Say: no more red, no more black

Red Noor
Holy Hoor
Symbol of
creation's beauty,

I see His
al-Wasi attribute
in the Mountains

of immensity,

in busy bazaars
catch a breeze
of His Name al-Muqsit

through mystical Azaan
Divine as-Sami
pops into my ears

Oh my,
when I

hold you
close
to
my
chest

Names mix
mine into yours
yours into mine

since
beautiful scenery
and horizons
can't give
my soul
the music
you do,

wouldn't
it be
disloyalty to
Allah

If I now
do not talk of
Him in my
greatest experience:
You

you, who have

'An hour's
thought
is better
than a year
praising.'

PROPHET
Muhammad
صلى الله عليه وسلم

Worship
and adoring
Beauty is
not enough.
Use your
intellect to
unlock
love's
meaning.
Zoom to
Reality in
the blink of
an eye.
Traverse
the distance
of galaxies
instantly.
For mind
accelerates
faster than
even the
space
vehicles of
the fiery
Jinn.

115   a Sufi Love Story

Have brought
Blue oceans
Crashing into
My heart

heart?
It no longer exists
Don't ever let me

Tell you more

Black tears fall across her face as she reddens the water this time by dipping her fingernail into the cup.

The waiting Angel whispers into her right ear,

Allah's too Perfect
To be seen in Himself,

when Musa aleyhis-salam
tried,
he fainted,

we witness Allah
through symbolic energizers.

The human
Ibn Al-Arabi explained
since 'women were
made lovable to the
Prophet' sal-Allah

women therefore
Allah beautified

and in the activity
with the two involved

there isn't receiving
but giving too

hence Black and Red
the individual and the non-individual

'Women are the twin halves of men.'
PROPHET Muhammad صلى الله عليه وسلم

The yin and yang of Love's interplay creates a Unity. Woman is 0.5 Man is 0.5. Together they become 1. The search is not for passionate pleasure but the lost half of that which broke away. Positive and negative together create electric lightning baraka.

*are oblitered so
that all that remains*

is

capacity...

*in
such
emptiness*

*your selves
no longer
veil
Allah*

The Angel hesitates, then places the red drink upon the lips of kalandar. Her song strings into his heart and awakens his passion:

*Do tell me more,
Uncover your
thoughts as
Western pose
If it's the season
of winter
You're my
Eastern snow rose
Whose inner
Allah al-Alim knows*

*Restore to your singular Self
a you-ness
that's entirely
a me-ness*

*The physics of life
is simple:
we were One, once,*

'The world
is a
magician
greater
than Harut
and Marut,
and you
should
avoid it.'

PROPHET
Muhammad
ﷺ

Harut and Marut were the Angels who introduced spell-magic to humanity. The world's lips are illusions. Take source-love from the One Beloved. These streets and suburbs are built upon a revolving earth. Fleeting dunya is an animation. Swiftly recognise the archetype and be snappy to abstain from the fleeting.

'Richness is
not from an
abundance
of worldly
goods but
from a
content
heart.'

PROPHET
Muhammad
ﷺ

You need
own only
one
cushion.
Make room
for your
Beloved
and sit
content, for
both of you
have what
none other
has:

holistic
peace

*not in another clime,
nor another life...*

*We were in essence
a unique individual*

*then Allah separated
us...split us in pieces:*

*'It is He who created you from one soul
and made from it its spouse that
he might rest in her.'* (Qur'an 7:189)

*I find my rest
where*

*you find
yours*

*we gaze into each other
maddened
our hands grab,
puzzled*

*Yet, it is in the quiet embrace of
Moment*

*The first reality with a Divine
Presence*

*begins to beam...
growing laser-flowers*

*my breaths tie you down
revealing your inmost reality*

*for two breaths are uniquely one
an all-comprehensive
river*

*we become the black tar
and the alchemy*

we become the seer and

the seen

we become the toucher
and the touched

both sides of the barzakh
have met

the isthmus is finally a circle
in us.

Allah is.

She lifts her head and can see her red light still glowing in his chest. The green has left them. They are clear transparent bodies admixed with each other's black and red souls. She sips again and catches his falling senses:

you are the morning rain
that wakes my moments

you are the dew
that refreshes my skin

you are the weather
that I try to predict

you have the face
I desire the most

you have the persona
I yearn to unite in

every motion of your blessed hand
I follow with trepidation

beam a love-smile
my way

can I
refresh myself with your gel

oh Symbol
shower me with your insight

'Verily, Allah is mild, and is fond of mildness, and he gives to the mild what he does not to the harsh.'

PROPHET Muhammad صَلَّى اللهُ عَلَيْهِ وَسَلَّمَ

Fragrant love is dispensed at the store frequented by those who are given to a civilised bent of mind.

(by civilized I don't mean you know who)

a Sufi Love Story

'Allah is
One, and
loves
Unity.'

PROPHET
Muhammad
صَلَّى اللهُ عَلَيْهِ وَسَلَّم

When you
centre
yourself to
your own
personality,
you
construct a
separate
field, which
like a
bubble
around you,
disassociates
cartoon-like
from the
feeling of
belonging
to the
Whole.

His eyebrows alter colour and his spices reach her:

at each zikr of La-ilaha-il-Allah,
there is only your chehra
indicating Allah Al-Musawwar

look outside when the sun is no more
you will find me

standing by
you

at dusk I guard your Palace
where, I work digging your gold

my body has reshaped to be worthy of you,
a head fit to be crowned your Prince

I have a door next to your throne room,
my constant cry:
there is no god but God

my subroutines churn out a program
in which you are beheld, cherished and spoken of

my thought-police constantly watch lest I
praise you as a goddess

outside your Palace
in the frozen winter clouds

I look for you
from afar

you make
life liveable

Download
my soul

as

I swim in the clouds
and find a winged deer

flying
amidst
the
fog

in each of its eyes
I see your curls

adorning your
cherished face

I can't say enough
to paint you adequately

you're too sculpted
much too wonderful

Making me wonder
How Beautiful Allah

Is...

the essential
has come
through

She gives the drink a glance that he swallows:

Your enchanting thoughts
encircles your gravitas

'Allah says,
I was a
hidden
treasure. I
wanted to
be
known.'

PROPHET
Muhammad
صلى الله عليه وسلم

This is the
answer to
the
question of
Life. We
are here to
discover the
gems and
jewels
hidden in
the crust of
today and
tomorrow.

a Sufi Love Story

'Trust in Allah, but tie your camel.'

PROPHET
Muhammad

Tie your goods. See Him, but see her too. Love the Actual Beloved, yet kiss the beloved. Shun not the illusory blobs of solidified vibrations that is the 3D plane of existence – rather shun thinking they are the ultimate things. Weave magnificent living here on earth, even though you know that your environment is basically empty.

Blissful winks of thine eyes
populate my emptiness

and all my

desires

You have made my night
a starlit movie
kiss

and each memory
of your mannerisms

tingles
in
my
mind

your gushing words
are a baraka spell

from which
I cannot
leave, oh soul of mine

I drop at your feet
drowned in tears

awaiting

the next chapter of
your unveiling...
so

hide me, oh
my baraka catalyst

I cannot convey
my real feelings

For my brain
is burnt-out

He replies with:

A portrait of your soul
hangs in my psyche

Your nightsky hair a crown
your purest skin a gown

the rose in your chest
enchants my future

the dots on your eyes
are nuqtay of His Qur'an

and the opening of your eyes
is the Fatiha to your Surah

the ayat of your resplendent face
Is a taweez upon my neck

My mortal thoughts
you turn to immortal

Shukr lillah

the Spirit of your ruh
symbolizes His Hidden-ness

amid the impulses I have for you
senses perceive Allah-Love

the bright spark of tongue
ignites my Namaz with meaning

the lingering pulse
of your Nearness

Oh
Noble
One

Allah is different to us

'Beware! verily there is a piece of flesh in the body, which when good, the whole body is healthy; and when bad, the whole body is ill, and that is the heart.'

PROPHET Muhammad

Allow yourself a floating love that cures your heart. A calming.

a Sufi Love Story

'Do not say that if people do good to us, we will do good to them; and if people oppress us, we will oppress them; but determine that if people do you good, you will do good to them; and if they oppress you, you will not oppress them.'

PROPHET
Muhammad

Those who know the Truth have such overflowing love that they are incapable of hate. Their eyes look to Allah and even the stars catch their transmissions of open love.

And He is One Alone

My comparisons are
Only because I'm in love

And can't see
Anything but Him

il-Allah il-Allah il-Allah

She looks into his eyes and melts her words on his tongue:

You are
Baraka steam,
You are
A sign
latent
A cuddly
sizzle
Of His
Creative Power

Your innocent moisture,
my aching desire

under thine eyelids
your farishtiyana eyes

when they open
my Eid begins

living in emptiness
loving in thought

swimming your endless Seas
Allah embraces my softness

let's join underneath crystal snow
later gather warmth from Him

taste me as a love-symbol
moist with the ether of word-dust
your eyes manufacture

the firelit flight of your movement
is in every breath I catch from your lips

shelter me in your magical arms, hold my weeping heavy
head
and may the baraka sky of your eyebrows shield my shame

Harbour your soul in my own black curls, caressing my
ship gently
and allow entry through the Kaba of my Face into your
jannat

Forgive my Reasoning
As it is tainted with love tears
of exhausted blood

in the oil of spirituality
I achieve the glory
of being with you

Inevitable fate
will bring us
a shiny future

if Allah wills it,

as the earth rolls
onto the night - I
await your presence

if Allah wills it

He sends mind waves crashing into her heart:

Cup your hands
Supplicate with me

'Desire not the world, and Allah will love you; and desire not what humans have, and they will love you.'

PROPHET
Muhammad

Once your Beloved has shown you love's shattering impact, you need not be desirous for anything. Who wants a candle when you can have light? Why settle for music when you can hear Eternal Resonance?

'There is a polish for everything that takes away rust; and the polish for the heart is the zikr of Allah.'

PROPHET
Muhammad

Wash away the daily dirt of stress and make ablutions at the stream of Love. Remind yourself of the Loving Centre of gravity. It will spread shining rays from the centre of your chest to every muscle and cell of your body.

Call
Upon He

Oh Allah as you paint this world
Does it become a mirror of You?

Homage is paid to You Alone

Oh Allah make me submit to
You as I should

Applause is to You Alone

Oh Allah in this mirror,
Allow me to taste your formless shadow

Appreciation is to You Alone

You have made her
Flow in my veins

Esteemed is You Alone

Give us the delight of your Jannah

Beauty is You Alone

Forgive all our lapses
And create a pairing of our selves

Rave You Alone

When we praise each other
Remind us to praise You

Praise be onto You, Alone

Allah, You Are
Unknowable to Mortals
Yet we slip
And make comparisons
Only as You
Are Beauty itself

Praise be onto You
Incomparable
Allah

You

And
Only

You

An eagle eyed angel praises Allah and bows down to the Adamic magnificence. His verses are moulded into perfect stars:

The secret to Beloved love
Is the promise of the Qur'an:

in shakar*tum* la-aa **zid** annakum
if *you are* <u>thankful</u> I will give you **more**

May all Lovers then be grateful to Allah,
For He has promised increase

Her sweat drops to mingle with his next sip:

A green meadow,
Hides a sun

with suckable chocolate
rays of brown light

we left our desires
He gifted our souls

A
Black
Taj

'People are asleep and wake up when they die.'

PROPHET
Muhammad

The real Love experience will be yours upon awakening from this grossly solid virtuality we call being awake. That is where lips are lips and the touch of the Beloved will activate your soul.

Mahal

You and I
are a pattern:
Our four legs
the square tile
of a Mosque

the mihrab
a void
to faithfully
discover ourselves
inside in

why not simply
tug me into
your living centre

place your little finger
around mine

quit
talking

for

Allah's beyond words.

Just hold me in your soul.

A newly arrived Angel is wondering what is going on. His friendly brother farishta answers his enquiring eyes:

A Black Horserider
rides by dawn
each morning
and listens to
the sound of
every Minaret

In his lap he
carries his Princess

'Be mindful of Allah, and you will find Him in front of you.'

PROPHET
Muhammad

He is Hidden, yet Manifest. But wait – has the secret realisation reached you? If not, become a lover. You have the propensity to receive - it's a certainty.

stunningly magnetic,
she glistens

as it flies from
universe
to universe...

Perchance you
may see these two
as they sail through
the universal nebulae..

Their steed is passion,
their movement calligraphy

their hearts
inhabiting
another
Reality

From afar,
the Horserider and his Red
may appear
in a
confused limbo

Go closer and
you'll behold
the truth of:

'That is because Allah is the Real, and what they
call upon apart from Him is unreal.' Qur'an 31:30

All nonsense on earth
Bizarre relationships

all contracts, possessions, blood-ties,
in themselves are worthless bits of data

it is feeling and inner perception of Allah
which is the significant gemstone

all else is worthless
fool's gold.

'If you all relied on Allah with due reliance, He would certainly give you provision as He gives to birds who issue forth hungry in the morning and return with a full belly at dusk.'

PROPHET Muhammad

Float and don't worry about swimming technique. The flapping of your wings in the orchard of His Love Garden will complete the circle. Have dependence and fruits borne out of guarded Love will come.

'Do not say:
If I had
taken this
or that step,
it would
have
resulted
into such
and such,
but say
only: *Allah*
so
determined
and did as
He willed.'

PROPHET
Muhammad

Love water
is
consistently
pouring
down from
the bottles
of Divine
Forever.

Oh my Angel-brother,
Go where you feel the Sacred,

Visit the assemblies of those
Who engage in His zikr

fly from whoever pushes you into this world.

Don't you see the drizzly
Green lights that I do?

In two connected hearts
you'll find

green spheres spinning
in wonderment

from the blackness of time
through red growth

two beings walking
barefoot in the morning mist

clad in loose cotton fibre
they are alone in themselves

each movement
waves of desire

the feeling of morning dew
rises from their feet to their

minds

travelling up through
their bodies transmuting

whatever ounce of feeling
or memory they own

as if in the alchemist's flask
slowly turning golden,

the green suns refuse to set
as utter peace revolves
upon itself

rising from the abyss of passion
to fly the heights of heavenly jannah

The Angel's radiance vibrates and flying baraka radiates out of the eye of each arching Nur-light. He asks a further question, diamonds do not have the colour of love's blood, so when will dark snow awaken the red in diamond?

The Angelic answer:

Deep within the ravines
and the hustle and bustle

of earthly situations,
Allah draws mithaal

likenesses from every
conceivable encounter

when one least expects,
He grants a path unknown

for his beautiful creatures to tread
upon the road to infinite-belonging

don't despair of
Allah's Leniency

His everlasting heaven
isn't just for show...

An exceptional diamond
cut from His own Hand

admired and stared by all,
desired by the entire army of men

continued to scatter her effulgence

'The best are those most useful to others.'

PROPHET Muhammad

Build a life that's based upon allowing the speeding flow of dreamy love to circulate. Leave aside the dull mayhem of the world's strictness and it's unbelievably claustrophobic regulations.

until the day a dark shadow fell,

*flakes of snow emerged to drop
without will into the diamond's path,*

*Red light
once ignited
inside
diamond will
never extinguish*

*and snow
from a
shadow will
always fall.*

Kalandar has heard this answer. He senses Noor's question is the same as his, so he asks:

'If Allah created two souls
from one soul, then why
doesn't He bring them
to remain in themselves?

The Angel answers:

*I can see a purple place, where a rocky ground is made
from water-lilies and the sky is a smile,*

*A water bearer is showing the way,
by pointing to a celestial sign,*

It indicates:

*'Had Allah united two souls permanently,
they would be so stuck in themselves,
that love-ishq would circulate
in their completion. It is in the arena
of separation that their hands turn to
creativity and service to humankind,
their feelings of love are forced onto*

other creatures and blood-ties,
indeed, in separation, you will
often find separated soul-mates
turning to Allah.'

I sighed:

'But what if Allah
is found in the very
act of union with
one's beloved.'

There was another
sign at the edge of
this purple planet:

Oneness is Peace,
After that
Creation ceases

The cup is now empty of all contents and their bodies are a mixture of red and black.

The main gate of the Black Taj Mahal opens, a white angelic beam sheds tears of gripping translucent light. Its weight attracts their souls. They fly towards it. Their spiritual hands magnetically locked together. A Mughal Throne appears.

The pair, swimming in the Graceful Baraka of Allah, alight upon the Footstool of the Throne.

Their wantings thrust forward...

Energies of baraka swirl as gravities of their souls collide. Their inner green fields are lush with the water of universal light. In the moon of their pupils they can view the beautified coupling as their sensations cast a red shadow across the Black Taj Mahal. Rubies devour diamonds in gold encrusted tongues. Forever scatters an infinite pleasure with knowledge of their unknowns becoming viewed. Over the horizon of their souls, liquid musk caresses their electric eyelashes. The steed is floating ever higher as the purple contact increases. Awareness lingers. Deepens. Fingertips haul their memories to be played out on the screen of the inner courtyard of the Mahal. Black

'Do not crave after property lest you should be absorbed in the life of the world.'

PROPHET
Muhammad
صَلَّى اللهُ عَلَيْهِ وَسَلَّم

To love ever more deeply, be grateful for those who you love and detach your soul from their worldly existence, by penetrating their veil of relationship to you. Once you do this, you will notice they are mirror images and their reality is temporal. And the beloved is not the Eternal One, but merely His shadow. Hold them in your arms and realise they are somewhere else in actuality.

marble glows an uncanny red. Vibrations become a paired scent of an uncarpeted galaxy. Everything harmonizes.

Like a newborn, their joined undifferentiated spiritual being floats to the surface.

It is neither Noor nor Kalandar. Meaning is distorted, as the senses no longer believe signals given about their surroundings. Their perceptive powers create something outside the box of convention. They are in the environment of each other. The outside doesn't exist. No such thing as a system, no world is out there in reality.

No assumptions exist of what once affirmed their separate entities as now, a part of what is Reality, infiltrates into their consciousness. Realisation encircles their presence humming: *To experience Reality become greater than self. Proper spiritual strength ensues wherever selfhood is lost.*

They are two in a highly abstract connectivity with an unending silence in a bizarre unearthly echo of a vibrationless vacuum. Emptiness accelerates where they once felt they were 'something' and pure He-ness bubbles into the screen of their totality. There is none but He. Are they observers no longer? Any lingering sense of godness assigned to their own souls in pride has been lifted through *La ilaha il Allah.*

At the deepest levels of inner thought, they have subconsciously crushed all notions of time and space.

The construct of difference, of a world having parts, is alien to them. Weird even. No such thing as an intelligible fact or sensible prediction can be had for them at this juncture. As they have split apart from normal human judgments, the construction of 3D solidity and image-orientated processing such as thinking and visualisation.

This is the plateau of without-station. Like an impulse caught in a stationary wave.

Under normal circumstances they'd manifest thought. But they are in simultaneous alignment. One particle, one wave-function, one mysterious amazement. A higher level of symmetry refuses perfect reflection as there is nothing to reflect into. Sacred non-space.

He breaks away. And the brilliance of her soul is detected. He doesn't want to pull himself away. There was a merging. And now the separation. Inevitable. Like smashing an apple into a trillion 3D jigsaw bits. He and Noor are two of the insignificant bits.

Truth buzzes: lose separate selves by entering into the state of Unity.

A colossal waterfall of jet-black water.

Then they see it.

The Black Stone. Crystal meteorite from Heaven. Pushed into the corner of the Holiest Shrine. The Kaba.

They find themselves as two, whizzing around the four walls of the Kaba. Refreshing zam-zam water raining upon them. She sees angels clipping her hair and then holds Kalandar's shaved head.

The Black Taj Mahal looms large in the distance. The heat of red roses melts marble and the blackness becomes space around the earth. Noor feels the zap of her soul returning to her body lying in the Palace.

* * *

Watery inscriptions on the virtual Black Taj Mahal:

'Life seems so real, just like the White Taj Mahal. However the Real is only reflected in daily living. So therefore the White Taj is the reflection of the Black, not vice-versa.'
Kalandar

'Our actions on earth have a bearing in the Next World. Between these two planes of existence there are a thousand fresh worlds to explore. In one of them stands a Black Taj Mahal. A refuge from the Loving One for the mending of hearts and the stilling of tears.'
Noor

'What I had thought to be an untimely broken love was miraculously cured in the courtyard of the Black Taj Mahal. It stands, not in imagination but in a space more Real.'
Kalandar

'Gnosis is my wealth.'

PROPHET
Muhammad ﷺ

Whether you travel barefoot or by chauffeur, do so with realisation that your heart is undocked refined love. Provision will come to you: never worry about your state in the world. Wear the gold of your soul in the twin diamonds of your eyes.

'Oddly enough, when you taste the non-Reality of this world, you come to another conclusion: that this world isn't *completely* illusory. Absurd as it may sound, this dunya, these magical 3-dimensions, are significant. This is the simulation that has a Real quality, as intentions and action in this White Taj Mahal world aggregate to what one finds in the Black. Despite the Black being more Real in grade. Allah's Ways are Mysterious.'
Noor

'When I visit the Black Taj Mahal, I sense no fears and no worries. My physicality isn't with me at that moment. So this is the lovely happiness when we die. I feel as if the Black Taj Mahal and the angels and all the *stuff* in the spiritual arena is one and the same. A cool warmth.'
Kalandar

'In the deepest waves of muraqbah, my wounds heal and I travel beyond this dunya, and transcend the Blackness of the Black Taj Mahal, zoom through the White Veils of Light and then to indescribable non-place. How can I describe music to someone who can't hear? All I can see is Allah, Allah, Allah.'
Noor

'We can easily infer from spiritual experience that the image in the heart carries more weight than a building upon the earth. Our imagination is the real place where great architecture is built.'
Kalandar

'Do not underestimate the reality of any thought you have.'
Noor

Al-Haq. Actual what-ness of why, where and most
importantly, who.

NON-FICTION

Meeting of Lovers
separated by death or distance
A Muraqbah meditation methodology

Sufi Muraqbah for the Completion of a Pair into Unity

'Moderation is the best course of action.

PROPHET
Muhammad
صَلَّى اللهُ عَلَيْهِ وَسَلَّم

Fear not for what you cannot do. Taste and kiss the air: feel the evening love. Destiny is written by the Mighty Pen of Allah. Blame not yourself for your lot in life – touch the hem of the beloved and enjoy the moment.

Establishing contact
Make your intention for Allah at the outset. Recall that love has been placed between two humans in a symbolic paradigm. The Sacred Being is the Actual Sought One.

Imagine yourself in the presence of the beloved and build a relationship with her on a spiritual level.

Believe in Allah, say Bismillah, then visualize yourself in the vicinity of your partner. Keep your eyes closed.

See the Beloved through the eye of the heart
Do not look for her face, unless you must. Use a photograph only if you're struggling.

Concentrate on her concept. Her spiritual presence is more real than her transient physical form. When you begin to perceive her, thank Allah.

Allow the contact to deepen

Move away from visualization. It has opened the correct pathway. Your spirit should be with her without the need for creative *self-visualizing*. Begin your conversation and relax in the moment. You are no longer in the world so worry not.

Receive and give love

Connect your light to her light.
Create compassion extending from your heart to hers. Both vibrate within the Divine word *Allah*. She must then concentrate on any of the Gentle Names of Allah, and he the Severe Names. Masculinity and Femininity are paired. Resulting in a physical symbol. Unite and receive the pleasure of the Other.

'Idolatry is more hidden in my Ummah than the creeping of ants across a great smooth stone on a black night.'

PROPHET Muhammad صَلَّى اللَّهُ عَلَيْهِ وَسَلَّم

There is no god but God – Allah is the One Beloved. Love not the form but the formless. Make not your earthly beloved a statue of worship. Nor create a physical or mental distance from the one you are paired with and the ones under your care. This road is very precarious to travel, but leads to vivid realisation.

> 'Who has hair should honour it.'
>
> **PROPHET**
> Muhammad
> صلى الله عليه وسلم

The beautiful Art that is your body and face require time to shine. There is no ugliness in your form – only in your inner beliefs. Work from the inside but neglect not the shield of your face, your hair and your body – nourish it and adorn it with what you can. Become a Love-bearer of Allah's Art. Glorify the Artist through your outward form. Not for public show or to be praised by humans.

Two differentiated humans become one unified being

Both of you are together because you were created as one. Allah destined that you would unite. When you sit, be conscious of your connection in the spiritual world with your other body.

Veiling Yourself in the Light of your Beloved

Is your love true? For if your beloveds are many, you have failed to *become*. Veil your soul's beauty from other creatures lest multiplicity enter. Keep her in mind when another beautiful face or figure approaches. In day to day life, keep her as the third person in the room, protecting you from the snares of Satan – his lure to make you fall into the arms of another. But in this process do not worship her. She is not a god. There is no god but God. La ilaha il Allah. She is the medicine; take it to become whole.

Even when you are driving, running, surfing the net, texting or washing up, you will be with your soul partner as both you and your human partner on this earth, share one soul. Two bodies but one heart.

'There are as many ways to Allah as there are created souls.'

PROPHET
Muhammad
ﷺ

Oh generous human with effortless manners! You know you will be meeting Allah, thus you are more transparent than clear glass.

Annihilation in your lover can be the first step of the actual annihilation in Him. The *fana*[24] is felt and perceived and not an academic term. Don't define it. Be! And live in the moment. Once obliterated you realize that you no longer have a self. That your former 'me-ness' was an illusion.
Make fresh wudu ablution and pray two rakats to thank the Almighty for the experience of Oneness.

* * *

Two people are always connected
We are all one blob and together already – difference in distance is illusory

'Help those in sorrow and guide those who have lost their way.'

PROPHET Muhammad

Always carry an invisible umbrella of empathetic love, as around you are heartbroken disconsolate individuals. Make sure that as you help them, your heart remains happy-in-love and not distressed by their plight.

It may appear that two people who are far from each other cannot merge whilst they are apart. However, there is scientific thinking that suggests our concept of space and hence, distance, is a mental rather than a physical construct.

The universe is a totality in itself. It's not a lot of parts independent of another. The Big Bang theorem indicates that we were joined at the beginning. If all was fused together primordially, then this cosmos is a soup containing parts of a whole and not unrelated bits. Modern physicists refer to this as the 'Field'. Underlying field. Unified field. By this they mean that there is an *interconnectedness* in place.

The Qur'an informs us that our universe was one whole and then Allah broke it.[25] And Surah al-Mulk alludes to 'pillars we can't see'. So there is a structure and an unfathomable invisible Oneness. No 'out there' or 'in here.'

We are connected to each other. We're not really individuals. If we were truly independent beings, we wouldn't have the urge to love anyone or the capacity of empathy. We wouldn't marvel at a flower or communicate. That Allah has managed to create us as having individualities is astonishing. We are connected at a more deeper level with our soul-partner as the Qur'an indicates, two souls were created from a unity.

Two people at separate locations can communicate

Telepathy is always occurring. But as we don't pay attention to all information our souls attract, we miss most of it. Scientifically, we know that thought-waves of one person can travel over enormous distances and be picked up by another human being. So the brain is always receiving packets of information.

We are all connected to the *Nafs al-kulliya* – Universal Soul. We draw strength from it. To become tiger*like*, we can receive tiger*ness* from the *Nafs al-kulliya* and through it we also get peaceful serenity by harmonizing with flowers. Thus for instance we have similar brains to animals and plant features, not because we evolved from them, but because we all live in the same cosmologic plane. The creation we are part of is a patterning drawn from the *Nafs al-kulliya* of this phenomenal world. So when we think or act, we affect the *Nafs al-kulliya* and in turn, this can affect another part of creation.

Each human being emits mind-waves and a recipient who is 'tuned in' can receive these waves. If you know about resonance, you'll understand how frequencies reproduce information-waves far from the source.

If both minds are connected to an identical frequency, communication occurs. All senses can be involved when creating an identical vibration. Both could visualise an identical colour, eat herbs from one plant, feel a snapped strand of hair and smell exactly the same fragrance. The experiences do need to be uncommon and exclusive. So for instance, to create a unique scent, a particular mixture of say Jasmine, Rose, Musk and Sandalwood essence would create a distinctive, one-of-a-kind signature frequency. If both emit this fragrance, they would be near in resonance however far apart they may be in physical terms.

With thought we can connect to the beloved

This universe is affected by our thoughts. Quantum physicists have demonstrated the influence of the Observer on events. There are even experimental results suggesting that the mere act of looking at something can change its nature.

The Qur'an gives human beings a unique role in the universe. Humanity acts as a powerful Trustee. We are each a *Khalifah* of the earth. The Qur'an mentions pre-Adamic man. Before Adam came to Earth, this humanoid would shed blood on the surface of our planet. But Adam and his children would be different. They would be blessed with an altogether different nature that even the Angels couldn't fathom.

So both from the Qur'anic and scientific points of view, humans have been given the quality of imposing their thoughts upon the world. So two lovers can create a connection as atoms of the dunya respond to their will.

'It is more beloved to me that I walk with my brother in his time of need than stay secluded in the mosque for a month.'

PROPHET Muhammad

The path towards the Divine has been perfumed by soul-nectar. More intense than rose, jasmine and tulip. How can uplifting love confine itself when nearby streets are afflicted and miserable?

'Every important matter which is not begun by an expression of praise to Allah is maimed.'

PROPHET
Muhammad

This is the baraka shaft around which all wheels of success rotate. When the Divine isn't applauded and referenced, the debris of gloom follows. Those who are in love, see nothing but the name of the beloved. They wear the necklace of their love as an honoured emblem in the deepest part of their psyche.

Thought can give birth to phenomena. *What one visualises, mashAllah materialises.* We can also influence our communities as a sub-field penetrates each 'tribe'. Allah does not change the condition of a people until they change what is in their hearts. And research has shown that random number generators become less random through collective thoughts of communities. Thought waves exist. They bounce and reverberate. Control your thinking and your oscillations will create pathways connecting the pair of you.

The meeting of two souls are the meetings of real actualities
The soul is more real than the body

Our material world is actually empty. This may sound wrong or downright stupid. But science of the atom is showing that is simply just vibration, there is nothing 'solid.' *It just appears thus.* We are all condensed theoretical mists. Our realities have somehow been compacted to fit the body.
The Qur'an provides the example of sleep as the lesser death. *The roaming around of the soul away from its body.* As science searches for dunyavi patterns, its infrastructure naturally does not lend itself to 'discovering' the soul. However, as Muslim Scientists, such as Ibn Tufail showed, the soul can be known by its effect. Think of the times you or anyone you know have had prophetic dreams, déjà vu moments, seen auras, travelled together in dreams, out of body experiences and other perceptive sensations.

The Divine Astral Garden

Love, Allah and Symbols

'Do not back-bite, and do not search for faults.'

PROPHET
Muhammad

Turn upon the love pivot of the universe and you'll catch fragrant breezes that elevate you materially, religiously and spiritually. If the fulcrum of your galaxy is gossip, you'll become embroiled in unnecessary drama. It seems like a fabulous sit-com whilst it's in play, but give it a few years and you suddenly grow old and die without tasting any nucleus of meaning.

The entire universe, including thought and fantasy is a projection. It is a garden full of wonders and delights. Every little container, whether a leaf or a hand, is full of symbolic goodness. The Key to unlock its meaning is to go direct to the source. From the keyring of Revelation, take the interpreters: Qur'anic words. Inscriptions divided into wordphrases known as "Ayah". Qur'an words are conventionally translated "Verses". But, Ayah means "sign" or "symbol" and in the Qur'an we are moved to look out for and interpret His signs. Speaking to us in a language, not of logic and grammar but of meaning and metaphor.

ISHQ

Ishq, or as it is wrongly translated, *passion*, is like a growing vine that entangles itself around anything it desires. It would crush it if it could. And, often does...

The hedge to the garden of Allah is the Shariah. It keeps the treasure of Ishq from rusting. *Whoosh!* When ISHQ arrives on the horizon, the secret of the Qur'anic verse, "I created jinn and humankind only that they may worship me," opens, for in truth the lover only cares for the beloved and at that moment of intense ishq, nothing else.

"Promise me that I'm only the one you love," says one lover to another.

The whole Universe revolves around loyalty. Oneness. The axis of created beings constantly spouting out from the hem of Oneness is none other than Rahmah of Allah. And the Divine Secret as contained so famously in the Hadith Qudsi, "I was a hidden treasure and I wanted to be known, so I created the Universe," hints at this. A "wanting" is felt by plants, animals, humans and particles so they can give meaning to this. So how else can one explain the wanting of a man to be loved by a woman and the woman to be loved by a man?

UNION

Joining requires a *medium*, an incomplete matter to unite with. But in the process of union, the corporeal body is forgotten and senses lost. Confusion and undissolved energies reign supreme. An untroubled surge of becoming something else with the Other. As if you are a blend. *Mixed together.* No parts remain, and even the parts of the other person you were longing to caress are no longer visible. They melt away. The curves and sensual features drown, as do the individual signals of erotic pleasure you were wanting to savour. Wholeness slams its heavy fruity jam upon the bread of your thought and travels right through your eager open pores. Skin on skin is more like salt in water.

Now this is much different to basic animal gratification, where bodily moves are techniques for drug*like* arousal and instant gratification. It is less about satisfying the sensual urge, as it is about merging with the being of the other. To attach your detached spirit with another after such a lengthy long separation from the Source, is a unique and exhilarating experience. Bodily contours, eyes, lips, skins, smells, feelings join and ultimately achieve the losing of the self.

The act of intimacy creates an establishment. An unbreakable bond. Having attained a secret moment together, a vista of togetherness opens between the

'Allah has revealed to me that you must be humble, so that no one oppresses another and boasts over another.'

PROPHET Muhammad

A crisis at the core of society is a bizarre tendency to stop loving and begin competing for a larger share of cake. The urge to show compassion is hard-wired in our minds. But the short-circuit of greed transforms natural benevolence into artificial malevolence.

two of you. This parallels the secret moment with Allah, forever connecting you with the extra biological feat of shadow actualisation with the True Being. The first step is difficult, but once a huge bus is thrown over a cliff, it doesn't need extra effort to drive it onwards. It reaches the ocean. The thud of waves will overwhelm it in submission, as it drowns into the blue watery peace of newly acquired depths of realisation. Bang.

Divine Union doesn't happen through sensual pleasure. It indicates it. And even physical togetherness is *non*physical as your senses deep within do the feeling. The experience is certainly not lust, erotic love, fixation or a diversion. Rather it arrives as a Boeing 747 through your front door, in place of the tulips you expected. Uncommon. Divine Oneness for instance does not permit the running around to different individuals or beings, seeking sexual or romantic gratification. "Getting it" tonight here, and tomorrow there, and goodness knows where next week smashes the pillar of Tauheed. Leaving smashed bricks of polytheism and multiplicity. Suffice it to say here, that "true passion" can only enter from above and not below.

People who unite in goodness don't do it intentionally. It just happens to them.

SEPARATION and the MOMENT AFTER.

As moments with Allah make the *fuqara* [26] forget reality, lingering love remains, and the ones in love with Allah find it difficult to cope with the world. Outside structuralism slips away from them and they walk around, eyes amazed and unwilling to comprehend what's in front of them. Only that

'Mercy is taken away only from the miserable one.'

PROPHET Muhammad

The windmill of your soul runs on tender love. It grinds the wheat of desire and its oven of warm-heartedness bakes the bread of kindness.

which they left behind is clawing away at their souls. The pain of leaving Total Presence hurts more than the pleasure of remembering His Intimacy. Yet their senses are confounded and they don't want to accept distance. Carelessness and happiness fight in their hearts. The incredible sadness lunges tragically on. The soul longs for the source, and wants the taste once more. Allah wanted to be known. Since He is the absolute target of our affections, the world doesn't give up the emotions of wanting from humans. It makes sure that people don't get what they want, so the wanting may one day be addressed to what it ought to have been addressed to in the first place. To Allah.

BEYOND LOVE

Ata transmits that he entered the presence of Aysha, and said: 'Can you tell us about the most amazing experience you ever had in the company of Allah's Messenger?' She weeps before responding, gains composure and states, *'Was there anything at all about him that was not a marvellous wonder? He came to me one night, and snuggled up beside me in my bed until his skin was touching my skin. But then he said: "O daughter of Abu Bakr, let me go, so that I may devote myself to the worship of my Lord." So I told him that I love your nearness, but I prefer to respect your dearest wish. I therefore allowed him to take his leave of me.'* Humans have not been created with two hearts as we are timely reminded in Al-Qur'an. Blessed Muhammad's time with his wife. Blessed Muhammad's time on the prayer mat. Both are two aspects of one worship. Many say that if you fulfil your obligations as a husband or wife then it's

'Avoid envy, for envy devours good deeds just as fire devours fuel.'

PROPHET Muhammad

It may seem natural to be jealous of all others as you wish to be at the centre of your Beloved's attention. Perhaps you haven't come to realise that Allah's Love is super temporal. Measureless. There are buckets of this wonder. When you see yourself thus blessed with baraka you need not be jealous of anyone. For you have what you need.

'Those who do not show mercy to our young ones and do not realise the right of our elders are not from us.'

PROPHET Muhammad صَلَّى اللهُ عَلَيْهِ وَسَلَّم

Have clemency. Look around you. Blink. Blink your eyes for a second. Blink again. Can you see presents? All around you are Allah's endowments. You too can be a parcel that delights those close to you. A person full of goodies. Gentleness is the outer wrapping and graciousness the gift inside.

meritorious. Little realising the import this could have, they only see it as an act fulfilling one's role. Allah is not only found on the prayermat as Allah is not just found in the act of love. Allah is beyond. In one of Rumi's tasteful metaphors, if you seek the moon in the sky, it reflects in the puddle, as you try to grab it from the water, it returns once again towards the sky. Since what you see in the nightsky is not the moon but the light reflecting from it, Rumi's metaphor couldn't be more apt. Who's ever tried to grab light and store it? You can't. It changes direction or form and disappears out.

"Allah is the light of the heavens and the Earth," we read in the Qur'an. Hunting for light, hunting for money, hunting for fame and love, hunting for our origin, we ride on the deck of passion. He is not light, love, beauty and all these wonderful things. Ultimately though, *and this is often forgotten*, He is not Qur'an, Muhammad pbuh, nor a headscarf. Nor the Kaba. You reach your destination and are annihilated into nothingness. The senses seep back, you peer out and, gosh... Your quest remains. You remain and He remains. You don't want a cure, the game is too sweet. Far too sweet. Packing up your possessions, plunging the Nurlit dagger to kill your self once more you await to be zero again. Ad infinitum.

THANKING in LOVE

I once sat with a group of Arabs and European converts under the desert twilight, as we all feasted away, one of them stood up to say: we've got two blessings, 1) the blessing of the food itself, and 2) the blessing of being able to thank Allah for the food.

We all dutifully applauded yet there was something amiss. For now, we need to move away from any hint of a mistaken dualism, which sees Allah and other-than-Allah as fixed entities and only puts Allah as a simple provider of food: food being delicious (not Allah) and we thanking Allah for the food, not thanking Allah for Himself. When you love someone, you don't thank him or her for her services, there is an innate thankfulness which goes on, and true devotional passion expressed without the need for food, presents and all that paraphernalia.

Ishq seizes every opportunity to quash your earthbound senses and take you to another world. Scholars, needing control mechanisms effectively cross out the heart's authority, fearing its urges may take people away from Allah. But in doing so, the direct track to Allah is crossed out and rubbed away from the handbook to God. Like castrating a youth for fear of him getting up to mischief; when he becomes a man, what will he then produce?

Although one must respect the efforts of scholars, and dutiful obedience is indeed a step, it's not the highest step. They've stopped at this station, noble though it is, it's a lesser station than that of directness.

MIRRORS

Muhammad, upon whom be His Peace and Baraka, said that the faithful are mirrors to one another. I see you and see myself. You see me and none other than I am reflected in you. Mirror images are only images. Yet how often we forget that the world is a conglomeration of images. Dreamy images of sound, smell, the visual and touch are carried and reside inside our heads and hearts. The sensations do not exist of

'To harbour positive thoughts is a part of worship.'

PROPHET Muhammad صلى الله عليه وسلم

Think positively and be constructive. Re-arrange the furniture of your heart so that it receives well meaning guests who are progressive. Is your mind full of pleasant and agreeable thoughts? If not, go and daydream of the beloved, and fill up with the Garden of Rizvaan.

'Your love for a thing causes blindness and deafness.'

PROPHET Muhammad صلى الله عليه وسلم

Love not things but the Truth behind them. The vessel isn't important. The colour is immaterial. Roses whither in time. What is left over is the perfume of soul. Even the conceptual and its abstraction has temporal significance. The Enduring One is worthy of love's arrow.

themselves as our hearts give meaning to these images. The whole earth, enveloped in ghostlike solidity moves us ever onward, hurling us into another episode of life. Dramas possess humans, and they would wouldn't they? They're images as well. Art, music, philosophy and other feeble attempts at catching the flavour of streetwise beauty only leads humanity to branch out, when perhaps they should be digging deep within. As Ali, may Allah shower his face with Baraka, said, *the disease is from you and the remedy is within you.*

Sigh. A sad tragic being looks in the mirror of a passer by and views his own sadness. Searching for that unknown button to press, the drowning being fails to realise that it's not the world that's the sea drowning him but the craft of his self which has smothered a covering (kfr) over the soul. What is there for such individuals to be thankful about? Thanklessness is synonymous with kufr in many Qur'anic verses.

When I was younger I would contemplate on Shaykh Sirhindi's allusions to this world as a shadow. Often it's hard to accept that this ravishing lovely world is but a mirror, but when one encounters the Source of the reflections and incidences, another delicious ravishing hurls stones, cracking even the mirror open. And what one is left with is...

INTOXICATION

Words cannot describe intoxication, but everyone wants to get high. Losing the world, severing connections, *even if the net result is temporary insanity*, belongs right at the top of the pleasure apex. Frenzied behaviour, jangled nerves pumping discord throughout the system. Hormones, catalysts and chemical reactions wrecking havoc inside you. You feel there are hundreds of bits in you, and your being-it-ness separate from these independent happenings, that once upon a time, in your sanity, you thought was you.

Many drug themselves into intoxication using alcohol, human bodies and hashish. The way of the enlightened spirit is not thus. This is insincere love, not passion. Ishq is so far removed from our society of gimmicks that few can really recognise true love, and when it happens, they think it should be something else. Music, alcohol, poetry, gifts, bright lights, holidays and drugs are not needed for the ones drunk on love. Muhammad, sal-Allah, the final messenger to humankind is walking along and he pokes his blessed head into a wonderful window where Aysha washes his Mubarak hair with her own hands.

'Those who are nearest to Allah are they who are first to give a salutation.'

PROPHET
Muhammad
صلى الله عليه وسلم

Magnets attract or repel. Splendid indeed are those who begin recognition. They are the people of value. Society is encrusted by their pearly magnificence

---

'Indeed from knowledge, there is a part which is concealed, which no one knows it except the Knowers of Allah.'
PROPHET
Muhammad

The great secret of all secrets. Crux of the matter. Unspoken Truthful Reality. Haq. Follow the pathways between worlds. Experience meaning in the intensity of sense perception. Become infatuated in Allah.

END NOTES

---

[1] *Jootay and khusay.* Shoes. Khusay are often worn at weddings. At some Panjaabi weddings, the Bride's family try to pull a shoe off the Groom. Singular: *'jootie' 'khusa'*

[2] *Jai-Namaz, Musalla,* Prayer mat. The Prophet Muhammad, upon whom be peace has said that the whole world is a Mosque. So any part of our planet is worthy of prayer.

[3] *The Panjaab.* Farsi word meaning 'Five Rivers.' So it refers to the 'land of five rivers.' The incoming Muslims spoke Arabic and Farsi, and as the origin of the name suggests, the cultural motif of the *Musalmaan* (Muslim of the sub-continent) was language. Though not widely known, the majority of native Panjaabi speakers in the world today are Muslim and from Pakistan. Panjaabi poetry is renowned for its spiritual message. Latter Mughal Badshahs (Kings) in particular were much influenced by Panjaabi culture.

[4] *Baji*: Older sister. *Bayn*: sister. *Ami-ji*: (from Arabic *'Umi'* my mother) Mother. Muslims continued to use forms of respect that kept within the spirit of their religion. Islam, being a primordial path, did not originate with the blessed Nabi Muhammad *upon whom be the baraka of Allah*, so the ji-suffix, used for respect was adopted by the Muslims of the subcontinent too. The Qur'an states that all regions have had a Prophet, thus all places on earth have some remnant of Divine Teaching, even if it has altered over the course of time.

[5] *Mehndi night.* Literally 'Henna Night'. Arabs introduced henna into India. The Pophet *pbuh* used henna to dye his hair and in his household it was used as a treatment too.

a Sufi Love Story

Mehndi night though is a custom rather than a universal Muslim
ceremony.

[6] *Gora.* (Plural goray) mostly slang. Someone with a paler skin
tone. Although it is not essentially used in a negative sense, and
can refer to anyone, its usage is to be avoided for the Prophet
upon whom be Allah's blessings disliked gradation, separation
and designation of people by skin tone. He has said that a black is
not better than a white and vice versa. Such words sit uneasily
within many Muslim circles.

[7] Muslims are urged to be a 'community of the middle way.'
Qur'an, Surah Al-Buqarah v143

[8]*dhoola*: bridegroom, *dhoolan*: bride

[9] *Nazar.* Evil Eye. The Messenger Muhammad sal-Allaho
advised his followers to protect themselves against the Evil Eye.

[10] *Ganda*: filthy.

[11] the spokenly poetic suffix 'sh' added like pepper to flavour any
word, *often creating a masterly emphatic negative*, is reminiscent
of the well know Yiddish mannerism of the same 'sh'.

[12] *bara bahi:* older brother

[13] *mureed:* student. The Sufi path uses the mechanism of master-
apprentice to take an individual from the grossness of ritual to the
sublimeness of meaning.

[14] *gadey:* donkeys. Donkeys are actually much favoured beasts,
not only in Pakistan but also throughout the Middle East. Despite
this, fools are often compared to donkeys. Though as Mulla
Nasrudeen often reminds us, the donkey is a universal symbol of
contemplation.

[15] In fact there is no such thing as 'coincidence' or 'accident'. All
circumstance is patterned happening. Universal Director and
Producer: Allah.

[16] *Kutay da putr.* Slang. Son of a dog.

[17] *Ullu ka patha.* Slang. Son of an owl. For Panjaabi replace 'ka' with 'da'

[18] *paghal*: mad. The Sufi state of intoxication is often described as a madness. A happy worry-less detachment from the world. It is meant to be temporary and natural. Do not bring it on nor revel in it whilst you are still in control of your senses if you think it's happening to you.

[19] *Oway!* A bit of a shout. 'Oh-aaay!'

[20] *Theek hae?* means 'OK?' *Theek hae* means 'OK.' The *Th* is not pronounced softly, more like a 'Tteek' really.

[21] *Kharab karna.* To spoil.

[22] ***Hadith.* This Arabic word literally means 'news' and is applied to words spoken by Prophet Muhammad sal-Allah. Whereas we use the word *Saying,* the classical Muslims would use the word *News.* From a purely technical point of view, it seems more historically accurate to confirm words we have received as spoken emanations from the Blessed Prophet as *news* rather than *saying.* It is for reasons of convention that we use the latter throughout this work. Simply put, collections of Ahadith must be looked at cautiously including the sayings in this book. We cannot verify that these are actual sayings, but we can say that news has reached us that the blessed Prophet spoke thus.**

[23] See the non-fiction addendum on p139

[24] *fana.* Annihilation. The Qur'an describes this world as perishing. To taste the perishable quality of existence, where even self is obliterated is one of the high points of the spiritual path as it gives sensory (if we can put it that way) evidence to the fleeting temporal ship of this existence.

[25] Qur'an 21:30. Modern commentators sometimes refer to this Ayah as describing the big bang. Looking more closely, one can infer that there was a state of a 'universal mass' and then came its unstitching. Look at the tip of your finger. Now look at the sky. Both were once one. Think of the curls of your beloved. That stuff was a part of you too. Each atom in your body knows each atom in Venus as they began their existence as one thing. And they do remember their origin.

[26] *Fuqara*. Plural of Faqir. Literally the poor. Not necessarily poor in land or property or dress, but they are known by their non-alignment with the gross décor of the worldscape - to them, a dinner party of the wealthy has equal status to sharing a plate of chips with a ruffian.

The Divine Name
Al-Ba'itho
(The Resurrector)
inscribed in the Black Taj Mahal.

a Sufi Love Story

La ilaha il Allah
